The Land of Lost Souls

Elle Klass

The Land of Lost Souls

Copyright©2023 by Elle Klass
Published by Books by Elle, Inc.
ISBN: 978-1-951017-31-6

Editor Dawn Lewis
Cover art Getcovers.com

Author's Disclaimer

REALM WALKER

Books in the Realm Walker Series
In the Shadows
The Land of Lost Souls
Hidden Passages
The Ring of Betrayal

Other Realm Walker Companion Books
The Origin: Marya's Journal

Realm Walker World Books – coming soon!
Love at Frost Bite
Accidental Ghost: Soul Catcher Vol.1

Other Young Adults Series
The Bloodseeker
Zombie Girl
Hidden Journals
Baby Girl

Realm Walker

1

Halsey burst into the dorm, her face contorted as if she'd robbed a bank, her blonde hair styled to perfection. She pushed the door closed.

Terra looked up from the book in her lap. "Did you get it?"

"Of course. I'm the Diama of Navarin." She unfurled her palm, revealing a shiny golden key. "This could ruin me. I have expectations to live up to. We need to make this quick. I have to return it before the Dean notices."

When the veils were strengthened with the fae potion, the tightening of the fabric between the realms woke Terra from a solid carbohydrate-induced sleep. At that time, she noticed a curtain – the entrance and exit to a realm – above her. There was only one higher level than the dorms at Provence Academy. The one with the cupolas that they kept locked.

She informed her friends, and since her roommate, Halsey, came through for her with the kiosk filled with commoner, or human, food she decided she would entrust her with "borrowing" the key to unlock the door to the stairwell.

After all, sometimes it was better to enlist those you didn't truly trust into covert activities. It put them in an awkward position, forcing their silence. Halsey, as the Diama, or princess, of Navarin, had a lot to lose if it was discovered she'd helped. Probably more than anyone else on campus. She was also a fae, same as Dean Salena, which made her Halsey's servant. It was good for Halsey they didn't plan on keeping the key longer than overnight.

Halsey sat with her "ladies" at dinner, as she always did, bossing them into waiting on her while Terra joined her friends in the courtyard. Other than as roommates, no one knew they tolerated one another. Nothing was amiss.

"Will you take Clyde?" Terra asked, practically stuffing the handle to Clyde's harness in Kinzo's hand. The first friend she'd made since coming to Provence City. He was an attractive male specimen of an elf. A day ago, he'd changed his hairstyle a bit and now wore two braids on each side of his head and tied the rest of it in a ponytail that trailed all the way down his back. His tall pointed ears interrupted the flow of the side braids but gave them a sexy touch.

She trusted all her friends with Clyde, her chocolate brown-footed ferret, but he liked Kinzo the best which meant he usually got to be ferret sitter when she grabbed her food. She hadn't brought Clyde back into the cafeteria since the white-haired ice dragon lunch lady caused so many problems about having an animal in the lunchroom.

She covered a microwave burger in a paper towel and cooked it, then grabbed herself a chilled coffee from the fridge. It was nice having a kiosk to herself and if she'd gone any longer not having commoner food she might have wasted into nothingness. She didn't want to push it yet, but thought a toaster oven would be a nice addition. Microwave fries weren't the same or as crispy as oven baked ones.

Nalysse, Kinzo's elf girlfriend – that's how she always thought of her – tickled Clyde's chin as Terra sat down. He ran his front paws through her long hair. It wasn't that she didn't like her, or was even jealous, it was something else she couldn't really define about Nalysse.

The Land of Lost Souls

There was a silly elfin belief that their long hair helped them communicate telepathically with plants, and sometimes insects. Terra thought it hooey, especially since she, too, only part elfin, could communicate with plants. Her short, bobbed hair didn't hinder her. It was at this point a one-way conversation, but once she learned to manipulate magic better she hoped it would become two-way. The plant communication class she was taking was a big help. She was curious about the types of things plants thought about. It wasn't like they had a brain; but who knew, maybe the ones in Provence and other nonhuman realms did.

Caspen, also an elf, his hair long but also super curly so it didn't appear long, swallowed a drink of something orange and set it on the table. "Did she get it?"

"Yup! We're on for tonight," Terra responded with a grin.

Meesha held her fist to Terra for a bump. She was a lycan: tall, dark, toned, and beautiful. She was also Terra's magic tutor.

Hyacinth sipped on her chilled blood bag. She always put a straw in the top. "Lights out at 10. Terra, you should go first and unlock it so we can file in one by one instead of all at once. We'd make too much noise, and someone would notice." She was the only vampire in their group, but Terra was the only hybrid. Hyacinth was also Caspen's girlfriend.

Extrarealm relations were frowned on, except with vampires, since they were infertile.

They all accepted each other, including their differences, even Kayln – a water or sea fae, depending on who's telling the story. All fae had a smug attitude. Kayln wasn't an exception, but wasn't smug in the same way as Halsey. She was a bubblehead, and generally not snooty on purpose. Terra figured it was in the fae DNA.

Terra set Clyde out a bowl of food then turned her attention to the group. "She's coming with us," she said, meaning Halsey.

Their faces didn't hide the disappointment. No one actually liked Halsey. "It has to be this way. The further involved she is, the less she will implicate us and the more she will help cover things up." Terra laid it all out.

Not a single one of them knew for sure what secret realm had a curtain on the fourth floor of Provence Academy, but all had a good guess – Lols or the Land of Lost Souls. Or, in the terms Terra thought of it: home.

She'd been in Provence City all of four weeks. In that time, she'd entered five realms, rescued Tania – a human who fell through Thraves as her soul was meant to be harvested. She landed in Blood River in Drakonia – home of the vampires. After rescuing her, she had to get her home, but

Tania ended up a prisoner of the vampires, eventually escaping to Thraves and finding out she was part harvester.

Terra and her friends challenged the Tribunal – a once in a lifetime event – and got Tania home safely. The caveat is that, as a harvester-commoner hybrid, Tania can harvest souls in her physical form. Full harvesters could only do it in their spirit form, which meant Tania now had to seek and save lost souls.

After dinner and chilling with her friends, Terra retired to her dorm to catch up on homework. Halsey was there when she arrived, doing what she loved to do – toss clothes on her bed to find the perfect outfit for the next day.

"I can't believe you are actually going through with this. It's crazy and you could get in real trouble," Halsey said, with a hint of spite.

Halsey wasn't worried about Terra getting into trouble. She was concerned that if Terra did, Halsey's part would be revealed. "So are you."

Halsey dropped the shoes in her hand. They clanked on the wooden floor. "I will not!"

"You will, but leave the comicay here. That's how they track us and spy on our memories." The comicays were sticky, clear gel things that stuck to their arms, a hair above the wrist. They worked similar to cell phones, but were more advanced.

Halsey blew out a frustrated breath. "I got you the key. You don't need me."

Terra leaned against the pillows smashed along the headboard of her bed. "No, but admit you're curious."

"Maybe, a little. The tiniest bit."

Terra didn't need her along to appease her curiosity, but to hide the crime. A Diama was a powerful weapon in her hands. "Yeah, that's why we're going."

Halsey dropped the discussion and, when 10:30 rolled around, she followed Terra into the hall. She left Clyde asleep on her bed. She took him everywhere, but wasn't going to wake him. Their room was only about ten feet from the door that led to the stairwell. Terra slipped the key into the lock on the infinity-handled door and pushed it open.

The entire school was designed to be inclusive of each realm except Lols. The door handles were infinity symbols for Drakonia and vampires, the walls sparkly lavender for Navarin and the fae. The banister was jeweled for Verboten and the trolls, and more. Everything was designed for everyone.

The coast clear, they slipped inside the room. Terra, instead of flipping the light switch which might alert others there was someone on the fourth floor, turned her cell phone flashlight on. It couldn't make a single call from Provence City which lacked cell towers, being in a different realm and all, but it still had uses.

The beam of light displayed the same shimmery lavender walls as the rest of the school. The wooden steps weren't floating like the ones that went to the first, second, and third floors. These were wooden steps smashed between two walls.

Halsey shut the door behind her. A voice in the hallway caught their attention. Halsey's face contorted in agony. Terra motioned for her to stay still. Footfalls moved toward them and the door opened.

2

Halsey let out such a long breath, Terra expected her to deflate like a balloon. Meesha, whose room was across the hall and down a couple doors from Terra and Halsey's, entered. Hyacinth behind her.

The four girls went up the stairs, Terra in the lead. When she stepped onto the fourth floor, she instantly noted a change in the energy. It pulsated like a heartbeat. She stopped after a few steps and spread the light from her phone across the room. It was empty.

Flashes of familiarity crept up her spine. *Had she been there?* Four walls and wooden floors. The walls weren't shimmering lavender like every other wall in the entire school. They were a drab, cream color. She went to the closest window and glanced out. A door creaked below her, followed by footfalls. Terra turned off the flashlight on her phone and froze. The other girls followed.

Caspen's voice split the eerie silence, "Hyacinth, Terra?"

Terra turned her flashlight on and spread it toward Caspen's voice. He and Kinzo stood at the threshold of the stairwell. Caspen, spotting them, stepped across the threshold. A ripple of energy forced its way through Terra, and again as Kinzo stepped across.

She didn't have any idea what that was about. It was curious, but so was what she spotted outside the window as she quickly beamed her flashlight across it. Thick green trees. Trees in Provence weren't all green, some had silver, bluish, or even lavender leaves. She stared at the green foliage and, in the distance, mountain tops. They weren't in Provence anymore.

She assumed the change in energy and ripple she felt was due to them crossing the curtain into Lols. "Take a look," she said, "outside the windows."

Halsey joined her. Her mouth dropping when she saw unfamiliar territory. "We're in Lols." A profound statement for Halsey.

Realm Walker

To Terra, it was home, only it wasn't San Francisco or even California. She assumed it was somewhere northeast, in the Blue Ridge and they were somewhere in Tennessee, Kentucky, North Carolina, Virginia, or any of the other states the mountain range sprawled through. The thick, bushy trees that weren't sequoias gave it away and the mountain range was much smaller than the Rockies.

Kinzo glanced around. "Shine the flashlight to the other end. There has to be an exit."

Terra did. The room was empty of any furniture and the other end was dark. Even the light didn't reach it. Terra walked forward, at a slow and steady pace, the light guiding her.

"Shine the light to the left?" Kaylyn asked.

Terra did, illuminating a passage. Nalysse, who was the last to join, said, "Come on." The excitement of the adventure filling her words and movements as she was the first to take a step onto a narrow, winding staircase that reminded Terra of an emergency exit in a hotel.

It seemed never ending until they reached a final landing. A door at the end with a deadbolt. Nalysse paused in front of the door. Glancing behind her for approval from the group, she flipped the dead bolt.

The Land of Lost Souls

"Wait," Terra called, moving sideways past her friends to join Nalysse. She opened the door and stepped outside, trying the key in the door. "It doesn't fit. Someone will need to stay behind."

Halsey piped in, "I will."

A silent groan moved through the group. No one trusted Halsey to be the one.

Meesha spoke up, "I'll stay too."

Terra felt the relief, as everyone trusted Meesha. Lycans in general were a trustworthy subspecies. Fae were snooty, self-centered, and generally not trustworthy; add that Halsey had the most to lose. She'd probably go back to the dorm and leave them all there, then concoct a story about Terra sneaking out of the dorm in the middle of the night.

Terra took several deep breaths, allowing the pine scent of the trees to fill her lungs. Trees in Provence gave off a eucalyptus-myrrh scent that smelled good but was annoying when that scent was all she smelled on a daily basis.

The air, wherever they were in Lols, was fresh and crisp and wet. The moisture in the air filling her lungs. As a west coast girl, she was used to dry air. A chilly breeze swept over them. It felt good to Terra. There were no breezes in Provence. She likened the place to being trapped in a snow globe.

Realm Walker

Hyacinth joined Terra. "I think we're in Virginia, close to Cahas Knob." Noting the surprised expression on Terra's face, she continued, "I grew up in Boone's Mill, only a few miles from here."

Terra had never asked Hyacinth about her life before she died and became a vampire, partly because the opportunity never arose and partly because she didn't know how difficult it would be for Hyacinth to talk about it. She was sure she still had family in Lols and imagined never seeing them again was painful. Every day since her father's death, she missed him. Even though she'd never known her mom, she missed her too, as she thought of the pink carnation tattoo on her ankle that stood for her mother's undying love.

Hyacinth stared towards the mountain range. "I miss them, but its better they don't know I exist. It would be harder for them to see me after burying me. It was a beautiful funeral." She paused for a moment to collect her thoughts. "I was nine and got sick. I was born with a weak immune system. A cough snowballed into pneumonia. My body couldn't fight it off." Her voice, even though sad, was filled with positive energy.

Terra didn't really know what to say, but she was rarely speechless. "I miss my dad. I'll never have the option of seeing him again hanging over my head. How do you do it?"

"I've seen them, but they didn't see me. Devan's portalled me a few times. I'm good with watching them sleep or eat dinner. My little brother is fourteen. My sister started college two years ago at Virginia Tech. I can live with knowing they are happy. I can't physically join them, but I can share in their happiness and success."

Devan was her adopted vampire brother. Vampires were wildly diverse. They were human before being given a chance at a second life. Hyacinth was a young vampire and certainly hadn't lost her humanity. The vampires that kidnapped Tania she imagined as older, with little to no humanity left. "That's beautiful."

Hyacinth smiled. "This is beautiful." Her eyes still fixed on the sprawling, endless mountain range.

Since Hyacinth was speaking freely about her human life, Terra had a question she'd been curious about. "Do you keep your names when you are reborn?"

A breeze carried a few strands of Hyacinth's hair toward Terra, tickling her cheek. "No. We choose our first name. It can be anything we want and our last name we get from our adoptive parents. I used to be Jenni Pham."

The name she chose fit her better, in Terra's opinion. She had a hard time seeing her as a Jenni. Her dark, straight hair, olive yet pale skin tones, and almond-shaped brown eyes, along with her upbeat personality, made her think of a flower not a Jenni.

Kinzo wrapped an arm each around Terra and Hyacinth's shoulders. "That view is gorgeous. Reminds me of Aradia, but with highlands. Turn around, though, and look at the view behind you."

The school. Behind them was the school. It didn't strike them odd at first until they realized they weren't looking at the school. They were in Lols, not Provence.

Down to the very last detail, the brick structure was a complete duplicate of Provence Academy looming above them. But only the structure. The grass, Terra noted, was overgrown and shared space with knee-high weeds. The trees hadn't been trimmed in years, if ever, and ivy grew up the side of the building. "It's a duplicate. The school can't be in two realms."

"No, it can't, but we aren't alone either," Hyacinth said, then took off at phenomenal speed, vanishing into the woods.

"Hyacinth!" Caspen called, then took off after her.

She was much quicker as a vampire. Elves didn't have supernatural speed. Terra couldn't let him go alone and shot off after him, stopping abruptly when she spotted Hyacinth's green shorts, and then her blouse. She collected the clothes, tucked them under her arm, and caught up to Caspen who stood frozen.

His eyes fixed forward. The sight sending shivers down her spine.

3

Alarge, red-striped cat, its paws stretched forward and head low, growled at a much smaller bobcat. *Hyacinth*. Besides incredible strength, speed, and increased senses, vampires could also shift into large cats, mind bend or wipe, or portal. Younger vampires generally had one of the three skills, but older vampires could master others.

Terra and Caspen stepped back. The bobcat was no match for Hyacinth. Before their eyes, the bobcat morphed into a human teenager. He twisted his legs and covered his privates. Terra glanced away, as he'd lost his clothes the same as Hyacinth.

The rest of the group caught up and stood beside a shocked Caspen and Terra.

"Where are your clothes?" Kinzo shouted.

The wild-eyed teenager glanced at him then Hyacinth, and nodded his head toward the woods. Terra tossed Hyacinth's clothes toward her. They landed beside her front paws.

She collected them between her teeth, glanced at Terra as if to say thank you, and sauntered behind the trees.

"Hold hands," Nalysse requested, one of her hands on a tree trunk.

The comment directed at those who were elfin, as they could communicate with trees. Holding hands, Nalysse on one end and Terra on the other with a hand pressed against the same tree trunk, all thought: *Please bring him his clothes.*

The tree stretched its branches upward, as if waking from a long slumber, followed by the tree next to it, then the next. It triggered a chain reaction. The teen's clothes were dropped from a low branch onto his dark, wavy-haired head.

They decided magic, not just low-level magic but level 3 magic, was present in Lols and dormant, which isn't what they learned in school. This conclusion made sense since Hyacinth and the teen were able to shift. That took level 3 magic. The instructors insisted

Lols had no magic and when one went to Lols they lost their magic and memories. They'd proven both wrong. No one had forgotten anything, and magic definitely existed. If it hadn't, neither Hyacinth nor the teen would have been able to shift and the elves couldn't have "woken" the trees.

The teen's name was Mario. He hadn't been spying on them, and couldn't explain what happened to him. It started happening in recent months and he didn't understand it or have anyone to talk to about it. He didn't live far away, and ran to the school when he changed because it was empty.

"The sun will be up soon, and my father will get up for work. If I'm not home, he'll notice," Mario explained. His brown eyes no longer bewildered, but pleased. He thanked them before going on his way.

Hyacinth sighed. "He's right. The sun will be rising soon." Deflated, she turned back toward the door they exited. "It's gone!" she exclaimed, running to where the door had been.

The door had vanished. Terra and the others joined her, feeling along the wall.

"Mario said this place is abandoned, why don't we just try the front door?" Caspen suggested, calmly.

Hyacinth wrapped her arms around him. "I'd burn without you!" She kissed him on the lips.

The Land of Lost Souls

Technically, if the building was a true replica of Provence Academy, they should be able to enter through the front, go up to the third floor and enter the stairwell leading to the fourth floor, therefore entering Provence. But they came down a spiral stairwell, exiting out the back.

"The door is locked," Nalysse said as she pulled the knob.

Kayln flipped her lavender hair back and blew on her finger. The sun peeking a smidge over the horizon. She drew a circle around the lock, then poked the middle and said, "Druppo." The door slid open.

Terra assumed the word meant unlock, or something similar, in fae. Hyacinth bolted inside as the sun continued its rise over the mountain tops. Caspen quickly closed the door while they slid the curtains shut to keep out the sunlight.

Terra confronted Kayln. "If fae can unlock doors, why did we need the key?"

A smug smile crossed Kayln's face. "Because our sigils use fairy dust. It lasts at the site for about six hours and can be spotted by any fae. Dean Salena is a fae. I also think Halsey wanted to be involved, after all, she could have opened that door herself."

Terra didn't disagree. In fact, she was pleased Kayln was siding with her in her attempts to involve Halsey. She wondered if she could enlist them both with her plans in

Navarin. Merla was a sea fae. According to her limited research, it was Merla who used strong fae magic to build the veils between the realms. Kayln was a sea fae and Halsey was the fae equivalent of a princess.

Her gut said she needed to start in Navarin's Lavender Seas if she wanted to find Merla's Realm Grimoire. It never occurred to her she couldn't cross Navarin's curtain, even though that made no sense since one could only enter the realms in which they had ancestry.

Halsey didn't offer, or even mention, fae could unlock doors. She wanted to be involved. Well, Terra had something else Halsey could help her with. She was sure being the diama had its perks, but it didn't make her a cool kid. Rebelling and not getting caught did.

Terra walked alongside Kayln. "The word you said, what did it mean?"

"Open. Our spells use the old fae language. We learn it from a young age, but only use it in spells."

Every day she learned something new about these supernatural realms she'd only just learned existed.

The building, structurally, was identical, but the walls were drab white not sparkly lavender. No cerulean, eternal teardrop flowers vined the floating staircase from floors one to three. The gemstones and bronze weren't embedded in the banister. The doors outside didn't sport the pickax handles and inside were regular knobs instead of infinity symbols. The septagonal room under the stairs was present but absent the flags from the seven realms. The dragon-lycan fountain in front of the school didn't exist.

The large, thick curtains in the entryway were creamy and tattered, but they blocked the light. Years of dust covered the entire empty building. On the third floor, they went left as they would to get to the female dorms. The boys were to the right.

Terra appreciated they didn't discriminate based on gender. That didn't save them from discriminating against hybrids, although they hadn't made a fuss and forced massed banishing of all the hybrids who came forward to support her when she challenged the tribunal.

Caspen closed the open doors as they reached the third floor, keeping the sunlight off Hyacinth. Terra admired the care he took to be sure she was safe and could cross without turning into a ball of flames.

A wave of relief, followed by anxiety, passed through the group as Kayln unlocked the door to the stairs the same as she did the front door. No one knew if the stairs would be present and lead them back to Provence. In theory it should, since the building was a replica. Crossing her fingers, Terra entered the stairwell behind Nalysse.

4

Halsey's annoying voice parted the airways. Terra never thought there'd be a time she was happy to hear the spoiled fae. As she stepped onto the fourth floor, the energy changed again. The heartbeat of Lols faded into the steady rhythm of Provence City.

It was Caspen's idea they didn't go back to their dorms through the stairwell they'd just entered, but through the stairwell they exited. His explanation sounded plausible and worked. They exited through the narrow spiral stairwell into the manicured courtyard of Provence Academy.

Caspen explained there was one way out and one way in. He imagined it was to make things more complicated and keep commoners from entering Lols and those in Provence from leaving or returning. It was only his guess based on his reasoning.

The harvester brushed his long, chestnut, wiry goatee. He thought of trimming it, but the shame of being kicked off the tribunal was more than he could bear. It was his own fault for conspiring with the slimy vampire, Bane, who'd probably got nothing more than a slap on the wrist, or even a promotion from Minister M'ra of Drakonia, realm of the Vampires.

The weight of Metford's actions pressed on his heart. He'd played along, keeping a secret from the tribunal. They'd lost someone during harvesting – a female teen, Tania. She'd not only evaded her soul being harvested, but fell through the veil into Blood River in Drakonia. Their realms – Drakonia and Thraves – were neighbors. The souls they harvested went to the Otherworld, a dark, dreary place, or Tranquility, to which those with pure souls could go.

Commoner blood drained from Thraves, realm of the harvesters, down Blood

Falls and into Blood River. In this way, they provided the essence of life to all realms, as Blood River twisted into each of them. It was filtered through rocks and clay sustaining, the needs of each organism.

He glanced toward the wall. A secret compartment held Tania's blood sample that Bane provided. Why hadn't he turned it over to the chief? If it was discovered he was hiding it, his punishment would be worse than training the young hybrid harvester, yet it was also a commodity. She was a harvester hybrid. It was rare. No harvester had been banished for ages.

When harvesting, they didn't visit Lols or any realm in a physical form but in spirit form. Procreation as a spirit is impossible. What gifts in the commoner realm did it give her? Was she able to see and interact with spirits?

Their training had only begun, and she hadn't done more than watch through holocalls the art of harvesting a soul at the time of death. What she would be doing was different. She'd be harvesting souls that got away.

A knock on the front door of his condo drew his mind away from his thoughts. Opening the door, Elin stood on the other side. The female elected to take his place on the tribunal. She was beautiful, with loose, wavy, chestnut hair that fell across her chest, deep emerald eyes, and high cheek bones. Her turquoise dress hugged her curves. Not only a knock-out, she was also clever. Was she here to rub in that she had his old place on the tribunal?

"My first tribunal meeting is today, and I hoped you could offer me some pointers."

Him? He'd been voted off. What could he offer that the other four harvesters couldn't tell her? "You are in good hands. I'm sure the others will give you pointers." He started to close the door, but she caught it with her hand.

"You were my instructor in my fledgling days. Harvesting isn't an easy task, but you taught me well. I'm proud to take your place, but don't think you should have been voted off. Teach me what you know, like you did when I was a fledgling."

Her words almost brought tears to the large harvester's eyes. She'd been a model student all those years ago. He opened the door and directed her inside.

Rosette settled into her seat. They had a lot of business to cover in the session. Two new members, the vampire shifter attack in Canida – realm of the lycans – along with the strength of the veils after they used the fae potion to fill the gaps. She wasn't sure how many realms Terra had visited yet but knew of at least one other – Drakonia. Her instincts said she'd been to more.

Terra was a handful, but also careful and conniving. She knew not to wear the comicay when doing things she shouldn't. If she'd visited at least half the realms, she should be starting to feel the pull and tug of the veils. Any shifts in the energy should be apparent. Refraining from that conversation with the blunt and testy teen was to her advantage. She would have that conversation with her when the time was right. For now, all anyone needed to know was that she was a commoner, AKA a hybrid from Lols, and her niece.

Brooke, the fae secretary of the tribunal, called the meeting to order, first introducing the new members. Elin, an attractive female harvester, and Devan. He was far more charming than Bane, who looked like the senator he'd been in his commoner life with his hair slicked back, designer suits, and shiny, expensive shoes.

Devan was cute with his twin dimples, short, sun-kissed blonde hair, and green eyes. Rosette all but melted when he spoke, his Australian accent the icing on the cake. In her younger days, he'd have been the type she'd have fallen for, only extrarealm relations weren't allowed as they could end with a hybrid child. Vampires commonly dallied with others since they were sterile and there was no chance of a hybrid.

He was also the vampire whom M'ra chose to channel through when the tribunal requested her presence. What did M'ra like about the young man? She'd chosen him above others who were older and more qualified. It was no secret that M'ra, the Minister of Drakonia, followed her own rules. They hadn't elected him. She'd assigned him to this post.

After introductions of the new members, the timid junior tribunal fae – Olivia – rose from her chair. "Any reports on the veils?" she asked. It was her family who'd designed the potion that mended the veils and, at this time, there was insufficient data on how long the mending would hold.

Maglesh, an outspoken troll, stood. "We haven't seen any more dragons, or others in our realm. The veil appears to be strengthened."

There wasn't a single member who could see the veils, not even a hybrid had the ability. The only people who ever had the ability were destroyed during the cleansing.

Lukas stood. "Any word on the vampire who entered our realm and suffered a lycan bite?" He wasn't truly concerned, but curious. The more he'd thought about it, the less likely it seemed a vampire would enter Canida. The consequences of a lycan bite were fatal to a vampire. If not a vampire, then who had the ability to shift into a large cat?

Ernessa, an uptight female vampire, rose. "All vampires are accounted for. None ill from a lycan bite."

Chatter erupted around the room. Was she being honest? Vampires weren't always known for their honesty. AKA Bane. They had to believe she was being honest. If there was not a single vampire lost or ill, then where did the vampire in its cat form come from?

Colton, a large fire dragon, cleared his throat, gaining the attention of the tribunal diplomats. "There is only one other place that cat could have come from, and we've sealed the veils. We need to find the cat. I suggest we send a team to Lols."

The eruptions louder that he would even suggest it. No one went to Lols on purpose, except the occasional vampire. Devan spoke up in support of Colton's idea: "I think it's a great idea and we have someone in Provence who spent their life there and knows it well," he said, referring to Terra. Vampires knew it well too, but they couldn't face the sun. Any trip with a vampire would need to happen after sundown.

Maglesh coughed clearing his throat, bringing the Tribunal's attention back to him. His yellow-plumaged tail above his head. "Terra thinks we treat commoners poorly. She thinks they should be represented at the tribunal."

Elin was young and new, but couldn't sit this one out. His proposition was deceitful and disgusting. "Are you suggesting we send Terra to Lols under the guise of finding commoner tribunal members? If so, we aren't any better than the lie that kicked two members off the tribunal," she stated, all eyes directed to her which made her a bit nervous. She'd taken Metford's place.

Ernessa spat, her words nearly biting Elin's head off, "That was different. They hid facts from us. Our job is to work together for the better of all the realms. They lost a young woman and didn't say anything."

Sweat covered Rosette's hands as she clenched them in her lap. Their lie was small in comparison to her big lie. It was for the good of the realms, she reminded herself. The thought didn't stop the sweat from drenching her hands and beading on her forehead. Neither the tribunal nor Terra were ready yet for the truth.

"I agree with Maglesh and Devan. The girl, Terra, knows Lols. She grew up there. This isn't a dangerous mission for her. We can allow her a team of her choice," Colton stated, emphasizing choice, his words as large and booming as his size. Dragons were the largest of the realms' inhabitants.

The third fae stood. "We needn't speak in code. We all know one of Terra's best friends is Devan's sister." The message was clear.

Devan nodded. "I'll talk with Hyacinth." He wasn't thrilled with the unspoken ask, but it was his job now.

No one asked Rosette. Terra was her niece, but he was also right. Terra was capable of taking care of herself. She'd been doing it since she got there, taking the comicay off and galivanting to other realms. A protest played on her lips as Elin, the new harvester, gave her the eye. No matter how hard she tried, the words wouldn't come out. Terra going off to Lols, even under fake pretenses, might be a good thing. At least she'd know where she was.

Their next business was the hybrids. The rules said they should be banished but, in this day and age, it seemed barbaric. No one had been banished to Lols since the tribunal was created.

Liam, the eldest fae, who rarely spoke, stood. "The covenant banishing them should be upheld, yet how many of us can send a single one to Lols?"

Eyes shifted from one member to the next as they searched each other's faces.

Realm Walker

Rosette stood, finally finding words to speak.
"Terra is a commoner from Lols; a hybrid.
We have welcomed her. This is a new day.
These young hybrids, it isn't their fault, but
the fault of their parents. Maybe this covenant
needs rewording."

5

Terra mashed the leaves in the mortar and pestle for the healing salve they were making in Alchemy 2. She wasn't paying much attention as her mind wandered. The vampire in its cat form that attempted to attack her, and Tania in Canida, weighed on her mind. She hadn't heard a thing and expected the lycans and vampires to be in an uproar. Mario, the commoner, was able to shift into a bobcat. Was the cat that attacked them a commoner? Had it slipped through the veil before they were mended and merely a coincidence?

Realm Walker

Her partner took the leaves she'd been crushing and mixed them into a dish with the other ingredients, making a paste. Evidently, besides communicating with plants, elves were healers. Meesha had said as much during their second tutoring lesson, but that was different than experiencing it firsthand.

Each day she missed Tania. They'd grown close and she'd developed feelings for her in that time. It was only the beginning of something, but that something was cut short. At least now she knew how to get to Lols, although New York was a distance from Virginia and there wasn't any transportation close to the twin academy in Lols.

Tania, as a hybrid harvester, was sent back to harvest lost souls since she could do it in physical form unlike harvesters. If she planned for it, and with a friend – Mario – in Lols who lived close to the curtain maybe she could get to NYU.

Class over, she went back to the dorms, allowing Clyde to run freely. In class he did well, staying by her and not getting into trouble, but as a ferret he needed to run and jump. She'd grown accustomed to not using his harness except during meals. It gave him more freedom to be a ferret and in Provence he couldn't go far. She took him outside onto the grass instead of directly to the dorm. Once he'd expended his energy, they returned inside and to the dorm. He needed food and water now.

She wasn't bothered anymore when she returned to the dorm to find Halsey was already there. In fact, today she had something to ask her about. More like convince her to do. Gwond, Terra's magic instructor, suggested it was time she visited Navarin in search of Merla's Realm Grimoire, containing the level 4 magic spell she'd used to create the veils.

Level 4 magic was dangerous and included sacrifice. She didn't plan on recreating the spell - ever. It was more she was curious. Gwond planted the thought in her head, and she felt inclined to do it.

Halsey was the Diama of Navarin and Kayln was a sea fae. Maybe she could team with them, and they could explore Navarin in search of the Grimoire. It wouldn't be easy convincing either. They were both fae, but not friends. Kayln couldn't stand Halsey's 'I'm the Diama and better than you attitude' and Halsey, well… she thought that about everyone. She was the Diama and would rule Navarin one day. Everyone was her subject.

Terra scooped food into Clyde's bowl and poured him fresh water then sat on the edge of Halsey's bed. The fae lifted her head from her book. She had to approach this carefully.

"You're a land fae and also the Diama. How do you monitor the sea?" Halsey, as a land fae, could shift into a unicorn, which she thought was extraordinary, although other land fae did it. Not that Terra had yet seen a unicorn.

Her goal was to trick Halsey into the mission. Getting the key was one thing. Halsey wanted the adventure, but finding the most powerful spell book in all the realms was a bit different. She might not be so willing.

As she expected, Halsey was more than excited to talk about how wonderful it was to be the Diama and all the privilege that went with it. "Of course. We have the scramblers which can reach the sea floor and ride along it, or they can push through the water. I can check one out, and a driver, whenever I want. We also have gear we can use to leave the scrambler. They're beautiful, the Lavender Seas. They are like their own realm within Navarin."

"Can you drive one?"

"Why would I do that?" Halsey said in revulsion.

Terra should have seen that one coming. Halsey didn't think about the things normal teens did, like rebelling against their parents and freedom. How did royalty and rich people survive if they never did anything for themselves? It was a mystery in every realm and not one to be answered today. "Can you take others with you?"

Halsey smiled a deceptively sweet smile. "Of course, but they only hold four, including the driver. Are you asking for you?"

Duh. Who else would she ask for? "I was thinking I haven't been to Navarin yet and I've heard so much about it and the Lavender Seas. I'd like to see them for myself."

"I can arrange it, but are you sure you can enter Navarin?"

No, she wasn't sure, but she was sure. In other words, she hadn't been there but felt she could like every other realm. So far, she hadn't met a curtain to a realm that didn't drop for her. Gwond's words gave her more confidence. He'd suggested she visit. Why would he suggest it if she couldn't? But how would he know she could? She didn't care. It made her brain hurt to think about it. "Yes, mostly."

Halsey screamed and squeezed her eyes as she doubled over in pain, not hearing Terra's words.

6

Terra's friends glared at her. They weren't thrilled about their new passports, or tattoos, for Lols on their chests. That was the way of the realms. Once a realm was entered and exited, the marks came. But how was she to know Lols had one too? It was the only realm they could all enter, and she came from Lols and hadn't had a passport. Not then. She had one now and was curious what it would look like once it was fully inked and where it would show. The realms were in a septagon, exactly as they were around Provence. It was essentially a map, so where would Lols be? In the middle? Above? Below?

Halsey hadn't been thrilled either, but when Terra placed Clyde on her chest she freaked at first until she realized his breath made the pain disappear. She hadn't been pleased either about them having to sit close in order to share his warm breath. When it was over, Halsey then freaked about the mark that would now be permanently stained on her chest.

Terra really hadn't any clue. She'd come from Lols and hadn't forced any of them to join her, not even Halsey, who could have unlocked the door without the key. Instead, she "borrowed" the key. Terra was sure of one thing; she'd been born in Lols, that's why she didn't have the passport when she entered Provence. One had to enter and exit a realm for the passport to appear. She'd never entered Lols until last night.

According to Rosette, her mom found Terra's mom in Aradia, in Meradin Woods. She was an elf hybrid who looked elfin enough to pass. Rosette and Terra's mom grew up as sisters. The memories she showed her displayed a young girl running through the forest, playing with Rosette. They grew up more or less like sisters. Eventually, she fell in love with Terra's father – a fire dragon – and got pregnant. When that happened, they escaped to Lols instead of getting banished.

Realm Walker

Terra figured her mom was more than a simple hybrid, as she was able to enter every realm without hindrance. Probably why her mom had been left in the woods, abandoned. Terra, being a curious teen, did her due diligence, learning that powerful hybrids had existed once upon a time. They had powers from each realm they were a part of that somehow got twisted, making them more powerful.

Amber was the noted hybrid in the text she found. She was a fae-elf-troll-lycan hybrid with strong magical abilities, such as shifting herself and others, shooting magic beams from her hands, shielding and manipulating the mind to see what wasn't there. She was to be destroyed and her family sent to Lols until a sea fae – Merla – stood in front of all the realms and offered a solution: to put veils between them. Terra had no problem thinking and saying that others were scared of hybrids. Hence the banishing.

Dinner was a bit tense and going to the dorm wasn't an option right now either. Halsey needed time to chill and forget about the passport. Terra had six now. Going clockwise, starting with the 12:00 position, she had a dragon for Sier, a wolf head for Canida, a tree for Aradia, a gemstone for Verboten, an infinity symbol for Drakonia, and Lols was still a mystery as it wasn't fully inked. Two more realms, and she'd have been in each.

The Land of Lost Souls

Clyde chased after an invisible something as he ran towards the woods surrounding the school. The lavender, silver, and green leaves of the trees provided plenty of shade as she took a seat under one while Clyde scampered. She stretched her legs and leaned her back against the tree.

Colors spread across the sky as the fake sun set on the horizon. She lost herself wishing for a real sunset. Her eyes darted towards Clyde as a hoverboard thing flew towards him. She jumped to rescue her buddy, her heart pounding in her chest, but there wasn't time. In horror, she screamed, and the teen pulled the board up just in time then tumbled backwards off it.

Clyde scampered towards Terra and hid behind her legs, poking his head between them as the teen pulled himself up.

"You need to watch where you're going with that thing. You almost hit my ferret." Anger laced her words. What kind of person goes along on a moving machine of some kind without watching where they're going?

He dusted himself off. "Thanks for the hand," he said sarcastically, then hit a button on his board and collected it in his arms. He turned on his heel.

"Seriously, you're going to walk off? Not even an apology?" He was fae, with hair the color of lime sherbet. What more should she expect? Smugness was a fae trait. She folded her arms over her chest.

He turned then fixed his lavender eyes on her. "You're the hybrid girl."

That was authentic. "Yeah, and you're a fae who nearly killed my ferret. His kind are endangered. One day they may be extinct. I'm sure harming him would cost you a fine and you can't even apologize." The bit about the fine she was sure didn't apply to Provence, but it made her words more threatening.

"To miss your little friend, I lifted my glider and fell off. You didn't even offer to help me up." His bitter words stung.

She took in his baggy cargo shorts and blue tank top as he spoke. He was right. He did get dumped off his thing. His 'glider' as he called it. She hadn't known what they were called. They were more common in Provence City than at the academy. "I was in shock," she said in her own defense.

"Bjorn. I'm sorry for almost hitting your little friend. Better?" His words bit and didn't sound sincere; however, they were an apology.

She nodded. "Terra." Of course, he already knew that. It seemed everyone knew who she was now. That's what challenging the tribunal did – instant notoriety.

"What's his name?" he asked, his voice softer and less snarky. Eyes on Clyde as he peeked his head between Terra's legs.

"Clyde."

He shuffled his feet. "You made it OK to be hybrid. I know that wasn't your plan, but you did. We used to have to hide, now we can more freely, be ourselves."

"You're a hybrid?"

"I'm a fae dragon. I don't have much dragon. My great grandfather and his siblings were fae dragon hybrids. When they discovered them, the entire family was banished to Lols. My great grandmother didn't even know she was pregnant. They hadn't even announced they were thinking of getting married. Soon after my great grandfather was banished, she realized and married another sky fae right away. The rest is history." He shrugged and dropped the end of his glider to the ground.

How heartbreaking. It was a kinship of sorts she felt with other hybrids. They were forced to hide part of themselves. The same as her. It was known she came from Lols. At first, Rosette had asked her to dye her hair and pretend to be all fae. Her mother was a fae hybrid and her father a fire dragon. Her mom was mixed with something else. A lot of something elses apparently, as she had entered six realms.

So far, she felt like she was holding her breath in wait for the mass banishing, but with each day that passed, she realized the tribunal wasn't banishing anyone. "I'm sorry about your family…" She changed the subject. "You're a sky fae. You're the first one I've met. Tell me about it?"

He lowered his glider and sat on the top, legs crossed. "Yeah. We live in nests high above the Lavender Seas."

She narrowed her eyes and studied his face, noting the green freckles dotting beneath his eyes and cheeks. "You're not serious."

He smiled wide, showing his straight teeth. "No. Some of us do live in treehouses. That's a real thing. My family doesn't. My mom is a scientist. She develops and tweaks potions… It's cool, you know, being a sky fae. We have extra keen vision and can note an irregularity as small as a tiny ripple in the seas below."

Terra sat across from him as they talked. Clyde stayed close to her, keeping an eye on Bjorn. She didn't blame him for taking precautions. She was ready to pick every fae's head that would let her. She twisted her lip. "Maybe you can help me. I was reading about hybrids, and I hear Merla's Grimoire is hidden at the bottom of the Lavender Seas." It wasn't exactly true. Gwond hadn't told her it was in the seas, but she knew Merla was a sea fae.

He chuckled. "Yeah, so the story says. Merla's cave is also said to be booby trapped. Other stories say it's hiding in plain sight, or buried on one of the islands. If I was to look, I'd start with the disturbnace. Us sky fae see it from above. It's a place where the water swirls together. It's a strange phenomenon. The sea fae probably know exactly where her cave is." He shrugged. "Fae can be testy. We are protective of our own interests."

That was intriguing and not surprising. The part about being protective of their own interests. Kayln was a sea fae, she could ask her and planned to. More like convince her to hang out with her and Halsey for an afternoon. She wondered if she'd share the information if she knew the location of Merla's cave. "Where is this disturbance?"

"Between Verboten and the palace. The elder fae say it has something to do with the roots of Serenity Tree. They stretch underground into all the realms." He shrugged.

That was interesting. She was an elf hybrid, yet hadn't asked about Serenity Tree. Elves were healers. What magical power was in the tree? It had some great importance to be on their flag and the passport. She'd save that question for an elf. "I'm from Lols, but I never heard of that or the Land of Lost Souls until I came here. It was planet Earth and we were humans, not commoners. My parents, they left here before they were banished."

Suddenly her mind pieced things together. On Terra's first full day in Provence, Rosette made a remark about her father not telling her anything. It upset Terra, but now she got it. Her father hadn't forgotten where he came from. Lols didn't make them lose their memories. She remembered everything from her life and, when returning the other night, she remembered the entire experience. Rosette knew that.

Terra had her mother's tiara made of silver leaves with a gold object in the center. She'd never shown or asked Rosette about it, but Terra didn't doubt it was elven. More proof her dad knew.

Vampires wiped minds. Did they mind wipe hybrids when they banished them? Her father wasn't banished. Why hadn't he ever said anything to her? Lols had magic too. It was different and dormant, but present. The vampires wiped them, then filled their minds with false memories. Hyacinth called it mind bending. Her brain buzzed with the revelation.

7

Terra admitted to herself that the Lavender Seas of Navarin were gorgeous, and the sky was a deep yellow, almost gold. The realm beamed in the colors of royalty. Not much of a surprise, the fae acted so entitled. The water deep, but not so deep they hadn't passed plenty of coral painted in a natural array of spring colors in their descent, which matched everything else about Navarin. As the water parted with any movement, it sparkled and glowed from the luminescent microscopic organisms in it.

She didn't share her thoughts with the fae that accompanied her. It was fae nature to be snobby and she didn't want to start or hear that conversation. Like the other realms she entered, she had no problem dropping the curtain and even insisted she did it. They shared mutual smug looks but allowed her to do it.

Kayln, as she suspected, had a good idea where Merla's cave was. She wasn't keen on sharing that information with anyone. Terra tricked it out of her. She was a bit huffy when she realized she'd been manipulated. It took teeth pulling to get the fae to work together. She hadn't been completely honest with either of them, but honest enough to get them all to help her.

Halsey, whom she'd been most unhinged about bringing on this mission, but realized she was also in some ways the most valuable member, as she was the one that had the ability to take them all to the sea floor. As a Diama privilege, she had use of the underwater vehicle she called a scrambler. Each scrambler was also equipped with wet suits.

What she hadn't exactly explained to Halsey was that they were on a mission to Merla's cave. She hadn't wanted to hear the complaints about how dangerous that would be. After all, there was no proof her cave was booby trapped, or even if where they were headed was actually her cave. Sea fae lore said it was but, as Kayln pointed out, the story could have been made up so no one would find her actual cave. Fae were confusing to Terra. They didn't even trust each other or their ancestors. She was surprised they lasted as a subspecies. Terra wasn't concerned if it was booby trapped. She had the ability to see a map in her head and would know soon enough.

"We can't go in there. We can't. I didn't bring you down here for this!" Halsey's voice shrill even inside her bubble helmet.

Bjorn, who'd spent most of the trip annoying Halsey spitting saltwater ice pellets at her among other things, said, "You stay here then." He turned to swim further into the tunnel.

They'd made it to the entryway when the argument erupted as Halsey realized Terra's true intentions.

Halsey bucked. "Fine. All of you can go in. I'm staying here." She put her foot down metaphorically, as it was currently treading water.

Terra sighed inside her helmet. Fae were such a pain. "We have a limited supply of oxygen and no time to argue. I can see the layout of the cave. Ahead of us, the path forks right and left. There are chambers on each side."

"Merla's book isn't meant to be found. The magic in it is powerful! I'm not going!" Halsey twisted her body away from them.

Kayln, in her fae mermaid form, swam away and joined Bjorn, ignoring Halsey. Colorful scales covered her body as a shield. They shimmered like the sea. All life forms below the surface of the sea were similar to ocean life in Lols. They had the same basic body layout and gills. They were also colorful. A shoal of small blue fish swam between them. She wanted to touch Kayln's tail but remembered Meesha said they had poisonous scales.

Terra was done with Halsey. She could stay in the entry chamber and pout. She was getting a headache between Navarin's energy, that was like a yippy dog biting her ankle, and Halsey's stubbornness.

"I think we should split up," Kayln suggested.

Terra twisted her mouth in thought. "You can't see the layout of the cave and I can. I think we should stick together." It wasn't that Terra had anything against splitting up or facing unknown circumstances, but she was the only one that had her talent and decided to go with caution in case there were booby traps.

The light from their helmets spread over the plain walls of the cave. She'd expected more dramatic walls, with colors or glowing gems, similar to what she'd seen in the other realms, but this cave was bland and plain.

They decided to move to the right together. The picture Terra saw in her head showed the tunnels coming together at the end. She figured they could make their way around. Cautiously they moved through the hallway, pausing to the entrance of the first door. Nothing seemed amiss. Terra hadn't noted anything different in the energy, so they moved forward.

They entered without a problem. No falling spikes or magic spells that turned them into amphibians. The room was plain. No furniture or anything spectacular. The next room was the same, and the next and last room. The absence of anything that said 'home' gave Terra a pause. It didn't seem natural.

Kayln ran a finger along the cave wall. "It's not unusual for sea fae to live underwater, and in older times fae didn't make their caves welcoming to others." She dropped her finger from the wall and turned towards Terra and Bjorn, who stared at her apprehensively as if they knew where the statement was going. "In other words, they lived in their mer-form, but the absence of furniture is odd. Mer caves have kitchens, bedrooms, living quarters, and luxuries you'd expect in any home."

"What are you suggesting?" Terra asked.

It wasn't Kayln who responded, but Bjorn the air fae. "This cave is a dummy. A fake. Merla was powerful…"

Kayln nodded.

Meesha had been a great magic teacher. Terra hadn't forgot her first lesson wasn't about feeling and drawing on the magic in the atmosphere around her, but physically touching the ground and allowing the magic to move through her. The physical touch was more powerful still for her, as she was still learning and growing her magic.

She lowered her hands to the floor and closed her eyes, hoping she'd see more, hoping there was more to see. The floor was bumpy. Her palms rested on a thick, rounded line. Through her vision she didn't see anything more than she already had. She moved her hands over the rounded line, drawing over it with a finger. Her eyes popped open and she raised her head. "There's something below us!"

She couldn't see it, but her finger felt the line. She brushed away the sediment settled on the floor, Bjorn and Kayln helping her.

"What are you doing?"

The three stopped what they were doing and glanced at Halsey standing in the room's entrance.

Halsey swam toward them. "It was creepy out there, OK? It's dark beneath that drop off," she said, referring to the cave imbedded in a shelf with nothing but blackness below as she made an excuse for herself. To further justify joining them, she continued, "I can't go back to the scrambler without you. The driver will ask too many questions."

"Fantastic, you can help us brush the sediment away from the floor," Kayln said, as she turned her attention back to the design on the floor.

Once the sediment was gone, beneath them was a large, round, metal something that looked suspiciously like a door. Engraved on it were the words: 'Espessa meando calypa teor'. The three fae spun back in the water as if scurrying from a sea snake.

Obviously, its meaning wasn't anything good, but Terra didn't read old fae. "What?"

Kayln swallowed before gathering her voice. "Wrath will succumb those who enter."

Oh, Terra thought. "So, you aren't following me down?" she asked, not afraid of the ancient words.

This brought up a debate and discussion amongst the fae, as they gave a million reasons why they couldn't go down and how powerful Merla was. So powerful, in fact, her veils between the realms still held today. Not to mention none of them had any idea how to open the door.

Terra, ignoring their arguments, pressed her hands against the door. The energy stemming from it no different than the yippy energy all around her. She studied it with her eyes. It had to open. It was Gwond who got her started on this adventure in Navarin. She couldn't help but think he knew more than he let on. Would he put her in danger? She didn't think so. Was there a spell to open the door? "I think we can use some fairy dust and druppo."

Her palms against the door when the word 'druppo' left her mouth, the door beneath her hands vibrated, followed by creaking and rattling. She brought her hands to her sides and swam backwards. Her eyes widening as the door slowly opened.

8

"What have you?" M'ra asked.

Bane pressed his folded hands beneath his chin. M'ra didn't show herself to many and it was only her face under a veil that he saw. He studied the curve of her round chin, his mind drawing a picture of an oval face with dark, almond-shaped eyes, and high cheek bones.

She'd been good to him, though, after the tribunal debacle. He'd been true to Drakonia and that got him the plush position he was in now, as a personal adviser to Minister M'ra with only one job. "She's busy.

Today she took off to Navarin with three fae. I can only imagine what they are doing."

M'ra tilted her head in thought. "Navarin. That's how many realms now?"

"Seven by my count." M'ra's magic was powerful. More so than she let on. Under her cloak, he'd entered the girl's dorm as she and her roommate were fast asleep. He'd counted the realms inked on her chest. The only ones she hadn't entered was Thraves and Navarin. Today he scratched Navarin off that list.

He didn't waste the opportunity and pricked the girl's arm enough he drew a drop of blood, enjoying its taste on his finger a little too much. It would allow him to track her anywhere.

"And what do we know of her family besides Rosette?"

Bane raised his head from his hands and leaned backwards in his chair. "Her father passed away recently and she's from San Francisco. My search of her childhood home elicited nothing. Pictures of her and her father. Nothing of use. Not even a single picture of her mother."

M'ra had a special interest in Terra that probably wouldn't have come to her attention if it wasn't for the young harvester hybrid, Tania, who fell through the veil into Drakonia and, by chance, was happened upon by Terra who "rescued her". After learning

Tania's blood didn't contain that of all the realms, there was no reason to continue holding her captive. She was no use to M'ra.

M'ra didn't share why she was so interested in the girl, only that she was. A hybrid that could come and go from all the realms meant more than a hybrid. He understood what it meant, and why it was best they keep it quiet. His one and only job was to watch Terra and report her adventures to M'ra.

A salmon-colored wall behind her, she folded an arm across her chest as she spoke. "Devan supported the idea to send a team to Lols. It was fortunate that someone else mentioned it first. We need to make sure that team consists of Terra, and any friends she wants to take."

Bane no longer had any sway with the tribunal. M'ra chose Devan as the diplomat to fill his shoes. His father had served two terms and would have served a third, but he resigned with M'ra's blessing. Bane assumed it was because he was the vampire adopted brother of one of Terra's closest friends – Hyacinth. His position on the tribunal would keep him in line and maybe elicit information about Terra.

He glanced at the clock on his wall. Today was the tribunal's regular weekly meeting day and the meeting should be wrapping up. "What is the tribunal's proposal?"

"Diplomats. They suddenly need diplomats from Lols," she said with a maniacal laugh.

"How political of them. I guess Devan was given input on the commoners we feel would make a good fit?"

"Of course."

The idea was amusing. Send a child who followed no rules but her own to bring in diplomats from Lols. How would that work? The tribunal had thirty-five members, so there could be no tie. They weren't allowed to abstain. How would forty work? He chuckled with M'ra.

"Even better: the real reason they are sending her is to gain word on the vampire with a lycan bite. They wisely assume the vampire is a commoner," M'ra said in an amused tone.

"How do they expect her to find the vampire?" He'd been kicked off the tribunal for hiding the truth. How could they look the girl in the face and lie to her? How would sending her on a bogus mission find the vampire?

M'ra tilted her head as if surprised he hadn't put it together yet.

She cut him off without answering his question. "Be prepared for when she returns from Navarin," M'ra said in confidence as the holocall ended and Bane was left with his thoughts. Erupting in laughter as he figured it out. He loved his new position.

Terra peered into the chamber below, their helmet lights offering enough illumination they could see. The chamber was void of water and cozy. Below them was a flared-arm, floral, rose-colored sofa with a square wooden table. It appeared as something one would expect in a late 10th century castle. The floor appeared to be made of smooth shells. Nothing about it looked menacing.

She turned her head quickly to glance at the faes' expressions. The quick movement caught the light in a way that something caught her eye. She angled her head and stared at the entrance to the room. Tilting her head in various directions, she noted a film or veil of sorts that separated them from the chamber below.

Curious more than scared, she reached down to touch it.

"No, don't," Kayln shouted, grabbing Terra's hand.

"You see it too?" Terra asked.

The fae nodded in unison.

Bjorn glanced around and collected a large shell. His gaze shifted from one to the next as he held the shell above the entrance to the lower chamber. He let go and it slid right through the veil, crashing on the table below and dropping onto the floor.

Terra had no idea why the door opened for her, since she couldn't have much fae in her and didn't use any fairy dust as other fae did in their spells. She studied the glittery waters and realized the dust was all around them. It wasn't only the bioluminescent microscopic organisms but fairy dust everywhere that made the waters sparkle. Her mind again wandered to Gwond. Why would he mention the book if it wasn't something she should find or that should be found? The magic in it would do him no good as a troll.

The shell made it through, proving there was no booby trap. She pressed her hand against the veil. Unlike the other veils, it was cold and jellylike, similar to the comicays.

Bjorn pressed his hand against it and nothing happened.

"You're not a sea fae," Kayln offered as she pressed her hand against it. Like with Bjorn, nothing happened.

Halsey pushed them out of the way. "I'm the Diama. There's no way it will part for you and not me."

The Land of Lost Souls

Typical Halsey. Terra held in her laughter when the veil had no reaction to Halsey either. "I'm going down," Terra said as she scooted towards the edge and lowered her flippers into the chamber. The veil parted. It was more similar to a curtain as it was selective in who passed. She closed her eyes and dropped, aiming for the middle of the flared-arm sofa.

She landed with her butt hitting the edge of it, breaking her fall as she dropped onto the floor, her arm hitting the solid wooden table. She howled in pain, bringing her arm to her chest and grabbing it with the hand of her other arm.

Three faces with wide eyes stared at her from above, but she couldn't hear them. Their mouths were moving but with no sound. She waved her arms and pulled herself onto the sofa to say 'I'm OK'.

The chamber was nearly a perfect circle. An armoire and bed were on the wall to her right, through a sheer curtain. Behind her were wooden cabinets, a table, and two chairs. To her right was a desk, and straight in front of her was a bookshelf filled with books.

Getting around in a dry room with flippers on wasn't going to happen, so she pulled them and the head bubble off with a cringe as her arm still ached from hitting the thick table. She padded to the bookshelf and pulled various texts off the shelves. This would be easier if the fae could enter too. Why couldn't they enter? They were fae, as Merla was. It made no sense, but she had no time to ponder the complexities of the fae mind.

She needed to find the book. Merla's Realm Grimoire. One after the next, they seemed to contain nothing but normal spells. Nothing dangerous like level 4 magic that took sacrifice to make happen. She dropped onto the floor and pressed her head into her hands in frustration. Removing her hands, she noted something metal hanging from the bottom of a shelf where she'd pulled a book.

She pushed it upwards into the bottom of the shelf but, as if spring loaded, it dropped down. She pushed it again and again. Finally, she pulled it. The bookcase moaned and slid to the side, revealing a hidden room.

In the center of the room was a book on a stone table. Fae legend said Merla's cave was booby trapped. So far, she hadn't seen any sign of that, but a book undisguised sat on a table in a hidden room could home the traps others had spoken of. This could be the smoking gun that ensured the cave was indeed Merla's.

Tapping into the energy of the room; it was different, smoother. A hum. No: more of a melody. The notes carrying inside her head, playing on her brain, created a map and a path between dangers not seen with the naked eye.

She crawled along the path that circled around the room. If she'd gone straight for the book, the ceiling would have fallen around her. If she put a single body part outside the path, she'd drop into the abyss below.

Sweat beaded on her forehead and under her armpits by the time she reached the book. Above it hung an invisible cage that her sight allowed her to see. She rubbed her sweaty palms against her wet suit to dry them. It didn't do much good since she was still wet. She'd come this far. Wishing she had Hyacinth's vampire speed, she grabbed the book.

The cage dropped, just missing her hand. The pain in her arm returning with her quick movements. The ceiling opened up, and chunks dropped around the room. She tucked the book under her arm, gathered to her feet and ran, taking the same path she followed.

The ground shook beneath her as she leaped into the other chamber, landing on her already sore arm, and sliding along the smooth, shell floor. She collected herself and stood beneath the veil to the cave above, thrusting the book upwards in her hands, showing them her find.

The ceiling above her cracked as she set the book on the sofa and pulled her

Realm Walker

flippers on. Sea water from the hidden room flooded around her as she secured the helmet.

Grabbing for the book, the sea water lifted and carried it away. She swam after it. Grasping it with her fingertips, she pulled it towards her and secured it, then floated to the veil. The rock between her and the others crumbling as she pushed her hands and the book through the veil.

9

Terra dropped her backpack with the book onto the bed and sat on the edge. She hadn't even opened it yet, her curious side currently outweighed by her fearful side. The book itself stayed dry, even though it should have been waterlogged. Duh, it was spelled. The unmade comforter forming an uncomfortable lump under her butt, she leaned backwards, remembering the close call. Too close; even for her.

It was Halsey's hand that caught Terra's wrist as she helped pull her through the veil. Water bubbling through the cracking rock. The four retreated and swam towards the scrambler without looking back over their shoulders.

All she wanted to do was take a nap, when there was a knock on the door followed by Meesha's voice. She hadn't forgot about Clyde; she'd needed a moment to collect herself. She rose and opened the door.

"He's been a busy ferret, but didn't cause too much trouble." Meesha's hopeful expression changed as she glanced into Terra's eyes and gave her rumpled appearance a once over. "What happened?"

Terra invited her in. Clyde ran across the room, happy to be with her, rolling across the floor and jumping from furniture to furniture. Terra debated on whether she could tell Meesha the story. She trusted her, but the more she thought about what happened and what she saw, the more disturbed she became. The magic protecting the cave was so powerful even the fae couldn't enter. Almost like the curtain was made for only her to cross. She invited her in and closed the door.

Anything she had to tell her was private. She pointed to Meesha's comicay. Once she took it off Terra asked, "Can level 4 magic protect something inside a realm from those who reside in the realm?"

"Why do you ask?"

That's not what Terra wanted to hear and explain. "If I was to, hypothetically, go to a realm and enter a place that habitants of the realm couldn't enter, what would that mean?"

Meesha stood and paced for a few moments before responding. "Hypothetically, it could mean very old, strong magic was used to protect something of value that the protector didn't want those of his or her realm to get their hands on."

Of course. Merla didn't want anyone to get their hands on ger realm grimoire but why was *she* able to do it? "But why would a lowly hybrid, scourge of the realms, resident of the prison realm Lols, be able to enter?"

Meesha tilted her head back in thought then lowered her head and met Terra's gaze. "Not a lot is known of hybrid magic. It's possible the spell was meant to keep those of the realm out, but not strong enough to block a hybrid who has magic abilities from other realms."

Terra rolled that around her brain for a minute. It was true the abilities she had weren't like others'. Meesha, as her magic tutor, understood her magic better than others but she hadn't told her everything. Today, she not only was able to enter the lower cave through the cool gel-like veil, but she entered the room and saw a map. The dangers below and above visible, so she knew to stay on the path. "Could it be possible the magic was designed for a particular hybrid?"

"I think you need to be straight with me. You look like the destruction of the realms," Meesha's voice steady and concerned.

"I—" a knock on the door interrupted Terra's words. *What now?* she thought as she rose and opened the door. Clyde scampered beside her as she glanced at the troll on the other side.

"The dean needs to see you. Now." She wrinkled her nose, her tail plumage resting on her shoulder.

A million thoughts raced through Terra's head. The last time the dean wanted to speak to her was when she brought Clyde into the lunchroom. This couldn't be good. She glanced over her shoulder at Meesha. "I'll catch you later."

She picked up Clyde and he rode on her shoulder as she followed the troll downstairs to the dean's office. There was no way she could be in trouble for the day's events, they were too fresh. Halsey was still in Navarin, having dinner with her family. She wouldn't be back until later. Being a co-conspirator, she didn't think Halsey would say a word about the day's events anyway. She was beginning to trust her.

Halsey also promised she'd returned the key, which meant the dean didn't know about their excursion to Lols, so why was she being called to her office? She'd ask the troll, but doubted she knew. Trepidation filled her, as she couldn't imagine what she'd possibly done wrong and got caught for.

The troll opened the door to Dean Salena's office and Terra took a deep breath before entering. The dean glanced up from the papers on her desk and greeted Terra.

"That'll be it, please close the door behind you," Dean Salena said. Once the door was closed, she focused her attention on Terra who stood a few feet from her oversized desk. "You probably should sit."

Here we go again. "I haven't taken Clyde back into the lunchroom."

The dean's expression wasn't sullen, but curious. She ran a finger above her ear, pushing a few loose stands of blonde hair behind it. "I know. That's not why you are here. It's another matter entirely."

Terra contemplated sitting in the big cushy chairs as she shuffled her feet nervously. If she wasn't in trouble, then why did the Dean need to see her? "What is it then?"

The dean stood and walked around her desk, then leaned her butt against it. "The tribunal is asking for you." Her fuchsia eyes filled with concern.

"What?" trailed from Terra's mouth. It was the lamest response, but of all the things why did the tribunal need to see her?

REALM WALKER

As if reading Terra's puzzled expression the dean responded. "It was a surprise to me as well, but they didn't give me a reason. My job is to excuse you from classes tomorrow and have you escorted to Provence Square."

Terra's stomach dropped. "I have to wait until tomorrow. Why don't they meet me now?"

"As I said, they haven't told me. I'm not privy to those details. I thought maybe you might know something."

Did the dean actually say that? How would Terra know anything? It seemed everything happened around her. This was the hybrid ball dropping. That was it. They were banishing her and the others to Lols. That wasn't the worst thing for her. She'd be able to continue her human life, graduate with her friends but… The darn 'but' rattled in her brain as she and Clyde walked to the courtyard.

The 'but' was summed up when she spotted her new friends at the Academy in their usual spots at their table. Meesha with a plate of protein. Hyacinth with her blood bag. Caspen beside her. Kinzo and Nalysse sitting side by side, and Kayln, who stopped talking as soon as she spotted Terra.

"Meesha told us. What is it?" Kayln asked, as if she was in trouble.

Terra placed Clyde on Kinzo's shoulder. "I need food first."

With her bowl of microwaved mac and cheese with broccoli, and a dessert of jello with fruit chunks, she took a seat with her friends. Reading their expectant faces, she told them about her visit with Dean Salena and her fears that she and the other hybrids were getting banished.

It was Meesha's logic that made Terra feel a bit better. "If they were banishing you, why would they require you to go to Provence Hall and stand before the tribunal?"

Caspen followed that sentiment. "Yeah. Banishings aren't diplomatic. They'd hunt you down and toss you out. At least, that's what they did in the past. They wouldn't ask you to come to the hall in the morning, giving you time to escape tonight."

"Have you talked with your aunt?" asked Kinzo.

It all happened only moments ago. She hadn't even thought to comicay her aunt. She considered it now. Rosette was strait-laced and by the book. "No. I don't think she would tell me anything. Not if it's tribunal business."

None of them had any suggestion for why the tribunal might want to see her. It was only her they were asking for. She was the only member of Provence or the seven realms from Lols. Her brain hurt from mulling it over.

Kayln offered her a secret smile and a quick wink. They had a secret. She guessed that made her feel as though they had a special bond. They did, kind of, but it didn't give her any clues to why she saw the booby traps in the room. It felt like more than coincidence. Maybe Gwond knew. Would he be in his classroom? She doubted it, and should she trust him? He was the one who suggested she go to Navarin. Her mind was confused, so much weighed on it.

She left in a hurry after finishing her mac and cheese, not giving her friends an excuse, and scurried towards the classrooms, hoping Gwond would still be there, but the light in his room was off. Shoulders sagging in defeat, she followed Clyde as he scurried down the hall and towards the large front doors of the school. He needed to get his exercise before turning in for the night. Ferrets seemed to have an endless supply of energy.

He led her directly to the mobile unit or portable. Memories of Tania rested front and center. She hadn't spoken to her at all since she was sent back to Lols, and she wondered how she was coping with harvesting souls. It seemed an unfair punishment, even though it wasn't meant as one. As a hybrid harvester, she had a job, or a duty, to reap souls left behind.

She let out a deep breath and sat cross legged on the grass. Most times she avoided Rosette. She'd come to like her more, but still there was something about her. She'd lied, she knew magic existed in Lols. She had to have known. Clyde ran circles around her as she took her friends' advice and did the thing she dreaded.

A shock wave of elation filled Rosette as Terra's voice beamed into her head. She knew better than to get her hopes up too high. Terra was far from truthful with her, but not once had she ever contacted Rosette. It was always the other way around. *Terra.*

Hey.

Rosette tried to hide the worry in her tone. *You got the news about tomorrow.*

Am I going home to Lols?

Terra's words almost sounded sad, like she didn't want to go home. Life with Terra was a double-edged sword. She'd come to care for her, knew exactly what she was, but remembered she was also a teen who was still grieving the loss of her father. Rosette had to be careful. She was going to Lols but not home, but she couldn't tell her that. It was tribunal business. *No. Why would you think that?*

Why does the tribunal need to see me? Her head noise solemn.

Of course she wanted answers. Rosette couldn't blame her. She was probably noting all types of changes depending on how many realms she'd entered. *We thought about what you proposed and have a proposition for you.* She wanted to tell her more but couldn't, as that would break a covenant.

About?

That was fair. She had a lot of ideas and didn't approve of much. *You'll find that out tomorrow. Is there something else on your mind?* She really wanted Terra to come to her on her own and tell her about what she was experiencing. If she said anything now, she'd turn her away.

There was a long pause, as if Terra was deep in thought before she answered, *No.*

It was a loaded 'no'. There was definitely something on her mind and she didn't trust Rosette enough to tell her. The call ended and Rosette dropped onto the couch. "How do I get her to trust me?" she asked out loud.

The leafy plant on the table beside her reached out its branches and touched her shoulder for comfort. *You will,* it said.

The Land of Lost Souls

Terra followed her escorts, a troll and an elf, to the steps of Provence Hall. Her memories of the place were limited to challenging the tribunal. That's the other thing that set her apart. She was the commoner who had the audacity to challenge them, but it all worked out and Tania was returned home.

The members were in their seats as she entered the circular floor of Provence Hall. The flags of each realm hanging high above the diplomats' heads. Her eyes automatically drawn to the mural on the ceiling, displaying open realms and peace.

Rosette gave her a forced, pinched lip smile. That was probably the best she could do. Her brown, bat-wing hair casting a shadow on the wall behind her. Their conversation the previous night wasn't enlightening or helpful.

The cheery young fae secretary called the meeting to order. Devan flashed her a confident smile and offered a wink. Hyacinth hadn't told her he took the slimy vampire Bane's place on the tribunal. She was relieved to see him, but couldn't help but wonder if this was some sort of punishment to him. She didn't, at this point, have any faith in vampires, although she knew they weren't all evil. From what she could tell, their minister was.

The center of Provence Hall was a septagon. Each realm represented in fives below the flag of their realm. The eldest front and center, and the others behind. The eldest members from each realm stood. The eldest fae, Liam, stood, white hair flowing over his chest and small wrinkles tugging at his eyes. He cleared his throat. "You showed fortitude when you challenged the tribunal. Your words have been considered. You are the only member of the seven realms from Lols. They have been excluded. We are open to five more members from the realm of Lols."

What? Was this a joke? His expression not giving any signs that he was anything but serious.

He continued: "We have compiled a list of twenty-one candidates in Lols that we want you to observe and report back to us on."

Flabbergasted, Terra responded, "So you're sending me to Lols to vet commoner tribunal candidates?"

Lukas, the eldest lycan, responded, "Yes. That's exactly what we are asking. It's a big ask and you won't go alone. We want you to choose a team from Provence to accompany you."

The Land of Lost Souls

Terra's mind blew apart. Studying the faces of the elders, they were serious. She spotted caution, yet they made the unanimous decision to send her with a team… Were they all on drugs? That brought up her next question: "Who is accompanying me?"

The eldest dragon responded with clenched teeth. "You are choosing that team."

This was her dream dropped into her lap. She could go back home, look for clues that her father knew and remembered what he was, and maybe find out more about her origins. The more realms she entered the louder the voice in her head that everything was a lie. She'd be able to see Tania. "If you add five more members, the tribunal will have an even amount and there will be tied votes."

She bit her tongue as the words left her mouth. This was her fantasy, and she was questioning it. Of course she was. She'd learned to question all their motives. They weren't sending her to Lols to find commoners, there was some other motive.

The eldest troll spoke this time. "This is true. There are a few covenants that need rewording. They are… barbaric. I'm sure we can come up with a solution to a tie."

Terra wondered how close the vote was to send her to Lols, and if Rosette was in favor of it. Rosette's stoic face didn't reveal anything more than their dead-end conversation. She wasn't tight with her, but

Rosette had shown herself to have Terra's best interests at heart, even if her heart was a wee bit small. "I can pick anyone?"

"Yes. You choose. You have until day six to choose that team and, once sent to Lols, you will have seven days to research the candidates and meet back at the rally point," the eldest elf responded.

Her friends' parents weren't hard to pick out as they shifted uneasily in their chairs and wore fake smiles filled with concern. Even Rosette, noted by the shadow of her large bat wing hair. It was a democratic affair and, as sworn diplomats of the tribunal, they had no choice but to respect the vote.

10

"This is great. It's what you want," voiced an excited Caspen, his folded arms resting on the table.

Hyacinth flipped her long, straight, dark hair over her shoulder. "They are going to mind bend anyone who goes."

That was something Terra hadn't thought of. Of course they would. She didn't have proof, but knew they mind bent her when she was brought to Provence. The implanted memories as real as any memory in her head. "Is there a way to prevent that?" she asked.

Hyacinth twisted her mouth as she drew an invisible circle on the table. "Not that I know of… I'll do some research before we go."

"That means you're coming too?" Terra inquired, elated. It would be difficult, as Hyacinth wouldn't be able to go out during the day, but it could be very helpful having a nocturnal along on the mission.

"Yeah, of course!"

The group sat around the kitchen table in the portable by candlelight so as not to alert anyone they were there. It was their regular meeting place for all things conspired.

Kinzo placed his hand in the middle of the table. "All in, place your hand on mine." One by one, the group placed their hands on his. Clyde joined the group and placed his paw on top of the hand hill.

After their meeting, Terra stopped at the library. She hadn't had any time yet to peek at the Grimoire. She'd hoped to talk with Gwond about it and magic. Meesha was a great instructor, but he knew more. Maybe he'd be able to explain why she saw the map that kept her alive. It showed her the dangers. It ate at her, and there wasn't really anyone she could talk to except maybe him.

With the Grimoire in her backpack, she strolled to the library, hoping to find a quiet place to read the book. Lately, she didn't put Clyde on his harness but didn't think the librarian, although always nice, would appreciate Clyde jumping from shelf to shelf or running beneath tables and people's legs. She snapped his harness on as they entered the quiet room filled with an uncountable number of books.

It was late, and the library was pretty empty. A couple of trolls studied at a table, an elf rested on one of the puffy chairs with a book, and a familiar lilac-haired head with chunks of seafoam green, cyan, and brown rounded the corner from one of the long bookcases – Cat. She hadn't seen her in a while, but felt they connected. She too was a hybrid – a fae/elf. As with other hybrids, she'd mostly developed only a part of her nature. More fae than elf, she passed as a fae.

Cat glanced up from the open book in her hands and offered Terra a meek smile. Terra waved and waltzed towards her. Cat was a bit shy and not as snooty as most fae. "Do you have a minute?" Terra asked. She was direct, and figured maybe another hybrid had some advice.

Cat flashed a quick smile. "Sure," she said, her tone cautious.

Terra assumed it was her shyness. She looped an arm through hers and walked her to the other side of the library that was empty. "Magic affects us differently and I need someone to talk to like me."

Cat forced a smile. "I'm not sure I can help."

"I think you can just by listening." Cat was a sea fae who turned into a catfish instead of a mermaid. If anyone could understand, it would be her. When Cat didn't argue, Terra continued. "I see things and do things others can't."

"Because you're a hybrid."

"I think it's more than that." She glanced at Cat's comicay.

With only eye language, Cat understood and took her comicay off. They saved memories and she didn't want this memory saved so the adults could watch it.

"The other day I went to Navarin and was able to enter a cave." Cat's eyes lit up as she, like all fae, was proud of her realm. "The fae with me couldn't. I went down alone and found a secret room. At first glance, it was just an empty room except for a book in the center, but once I broke the plain, I saw it wasn't a boring, empty room. Below was a dark abyss filled with water and, above, the rocks were ready to break and bury the room in rubble. The energy played like music and a path was shown. I followed it and got the book. The cave collapsed after that." She completely unloaded on her and barely knew her. For all she knew, she'd tell the dean or report her to the tribunal, but she didn't think so. She was a hybrid who hid that fact. Keeping secrets is what she did.

Cat's blue/green eyes widened. Her voice low, "I don't understand."

Terra grabbed her arm and escorted her towards the back exit. She dropped her backpack and took out the heavy book, thrusting it toward Cat who was still holding onto the book she'd had her head buried in when Terra side-tracked her. She laid the book on top of Terra's open backpack and stared at the one in Terra's hands. Cat brought a hand to her mouth.

Terra laid it down on the table. It had a soft leather-ish cover. She wasn't sure what it was made of, only that it was old and spelled.

Cat ran a finger along it. "This is an ancient fae text?"

Terra nodded. There was no writing on the cover identifying what it was or who wrote it.

"You found this in a fae cave?" Cat's voice cracked with uncertainty.

Terra remembered how Halsey, Kayln, and Bjorn all scrambled like roaches when they read what was printed on the veil to the lower cave. She didn't mention it to Cat.

"Yeah. I think it's Merla's Grimoire," she mouthed, afraid to say the words in a public place.

They stood near and exit, and Terra dragged Cat outside so they could talk more openly. She lifted the cover and they both stared at the words, written in a language Terra didn't know but could guess. "Old fae?"

Cat nodded, without taking her eyes off the page.

"What does it say?"

Cat cleared her throat nervously and smoothed the page. "Follow the path…" the ground beneath their feet shifted. When Cat stopped, the ground stopped. As if to blow it off, Cat continued, "… of the footsteps." The ground shook more and marks like bare feet smushed the grass, walking away from them.

Cat's eyes grew as she stared at Terra wild-eyed and she thrust the book at Terra. "I can't."

"Why not?"

She pointed at the footsteps in the grass that appeared as she'd read. "The words are coming to life. That's never happened before. This book is dangerous!" She shook her head, shoved the book into Terra's chest, and turned on her heel and bolted.

That was about the coolest thing Terra had ever seen, so much better than seeing maps in her head. As Cat read, the words happened, and now she was freaked out. Terra sighed. Of course she'd freaked out. Unlike Terra, she was shy. Touching magic in such a way would make her uncomfortable. She'd catch up with her again and apologize once she returned from Lols.

The book being in Old Fae, she could ask Halsey or Kayln? Neither was a good choice, but both had shown themselves to be trustworthy. Bjorn maybe?

This was Hyacinth's first visit to Devan's house since being named the youngest tribunal delegate representing Drakonia. It was a light, green-colored home with dark shutters and a loft. The couch was soft, but a bit firm for Hyacinth's taste, and the décor bland. The only wall décor was a family picture above the empty fireplace.

"Chilled, type AB, as you like," Devan said, handing Hyacinth a blood bag as he took a seat on the chair across from her.

"Thanks," she said taking the bag. "It's nice enough. You could add a lot of color by hanging dark curtains and adding throw pillows." She gave her opinion, studying the décor of the home.

"My sister the decorator. You make a list and I'll take care of it. I didn't ask you here for advice though. Did Terra invite you to Lols?"

Hyacinth knew Devan well enough to catch the question within the question and answered with caution. "Yeah, and I'm going. I can take care of myself if you're worried."

Devan's dimple popped when he smiled. "I know you can, and I'm glad you're going." He paused, leaning an elbow on the armrest.

This was his serious look. The one he took on when he meant business. "The tribunal has a job for you while you're there."

There it was. The question he really wanted to ask. "You called me here for that? I thought you wanted to spend time with your sister, but you have a job for me," she huffed and rolled her eyes.

"The tribunal has a job for you. Recently, there was a lycan attack and a vampire was bitten. It wasn't one of ours."

She understood the gist. If it wasn't a vampire from Drakonia then it came from Lols. "Why me? There are better trained vampires to do this."

"I agree, but the tribunal agreed that you are the right vampire for the job. No one will suspect. They don't want to raise awareness around the realms that the veils were weak or that commoners were sneaking in."

They were sending Terra and chose to bring her. The tribunal knew exactly who Terra would choose and that's why she was chosen. Hyacinth stood, dropping the blood bag on the table between her and Devan. "No."

"The vampire needs you. Remember when you first started your second life. You had a family. This vampire has no one. If there's one, there's more." He pleaded with her soft heart.

Being manipulated angered her. The tribunal was an infuriating bunch; no wonder her father resigned after two terms. Now they were going to use Devan. M'ra too. She remembered clearly how hard the early days were and she probably wouldn't have made it through without her family, especially Devan. "Fine. What do I have to do?" She dropped back onto the sofa.

Devan was pleased how quickly she agreed. She could be stubborn; she was also loyal. Most likely she'd tell her friends at some point that she was searching for a vampire. "Find the vampire but don't engage. The tribunal will take care of that."

"I have one condition." Two could play the bargaining game. No one wanted to have their minds messed with, so if she was going to risk herself to find a vampire that may not even be alive any more, then they were doing something for her. Tit for tat. "Not one of us is mind bent."

"Deal."

11

Armed with a list and instructions to observe only and not interact, the group found themselves in a hotel suite in Connecticut in Lols.

They knew where they were and had car keys to an SUV parked in the hotel garage and the details of their mission and everything else. No mind bending. How Hyacinth had made that happen, Terra didn't question. Their memories of entering and exiting Lols were fully intact.

The names on the list rang no bells for Terra. As far as she could tell, they were everyday people. The first name and address on the list was in Connecticut, and Terra was the only one who knew how to drive a vehicle. She divided the group. Hyacinth, as a commoner before her second life, understood how to do an internet search and social media. She also couldn't go out in the daylight. She sent her downstairs to the lobby with Caspen and Kayln and Nalysse to dig up whatever they could on the twenty-one commoners.

Terra took Kinzo and Meesha with her to "observe" the first name on the list – Terina James. A quick internet search on Terina showed she was a single woman who won the lottery a few years back and invested the money into a small bakery in rural Middlebury, Connecticut, a town of less than 8,000 residents.

To invest in a bakery in nowheresville seemed odd. It didn't seem that with less than 8,000 residents it would be a thriving business, and why did the tribunal choose her?

Middlebury was located outside Nantucket and reminded her of Provence, with the old-style construction of downtown. The low mountainous backdrop and colorful leaves and freshness of the air made her a bit homesick. Trapped in Provence, there was no true sun or moon, no crisp, clean air only the constant, annoying eucalyptus-myrrh scent. The temperature never changed, and the trees didn't drop their leaves.

"This reminds me of Canida," Meesha noted as Terra parked the SUV outside the *Slice of Pie* bakery.

"Aradia too," Kinzo commented as he opened the door to the SUV.

The bakery had a few tables and a bar. It smelled like donuts and coffee. Terra's stomach immediately craved food. Pie, cakes, donuts, and pastries lined the shelves behind the bar. Large windows allowed an extra helping of light into the shop, and the cheery yellow walls made it feel welcoming. Terra pulled out a swivel barstool with a metal back and took a seat.

A server behind the counter immediately greeted them. Terra ordered coffee for all of them. She'd tasted their food and drinks; they were going to try hers. She remembered they explicitly were not to interact with any of the twenty-one, but ordering food didn't really break that rule, nor would they know, as they left the comicays in the SUV.

The server's nametag read 'Bonnie' so obviously not Terina. She nudged Meesha beside her and mouthed, "You have to order something."

Kinzo rubbed his chin, as if deep in thought over what to order. There wasn't anything vegetarian on the menu, but there were fruit-filled cakes and pies. Meesha ended up ordering a meat pie, which didn't surprise

Terra any, and Kinzo a jelly-filled donut. Now they'd get the experience of what Terra considered real food, not the stuff they ate in Provence and their home realms.

Meesha stared at the coffee and twisted the cup between her fingers before deciding to take a sip. "A little sour." Her lips puckered as she swallowed.

Terra pushed a few sugar packets her way and individual creamers. She was getting pleasure out of watching them explore her world. Kinzo grabbed a couple of the sugar packets himself and mixed them in before tasting the coffee.

The bakery wasn't crowded the time of day they were visiting. An older couple sat in the corner eating pie, and a young man sat at the other end of the bar reading a newspaper. She couldn't even see his face, only that his dark slacks and baby blue button up shirt looked masculine and like they cost a lot of money.

Bonnie the server dropped off their pastries with a smile. She was every bit as cheery and effervescent as the shop. Terra bit into her chocolate, cream-filled donut and almost melted in glee. She enjoyed her kiosk, but fresh pastries weren't something the kiosk could be stocked with daily.

She spied her company's expressions as they tasted their food. "What do you think?"

Kinzo rocked his hand in a so-so gesture, but took another bite, which meant he was enjoying it.

Meesha elbowed Terra. "The crust around the meat makes it a special treat. We have something like this in Canida, but the crust isn't as flaky, and the spices are blander. Not as much bite."

Terra couldn't help but smile in satisfaction. Tonight, she'd feed them all pizza.

A short-haired, middle-aged brunette approached them from the other side of the bar. Terra recognized her immediately from the pictures she'd found on the internet. The millions of freckles on her face made it impossible not to – Terina.

She smiled wide. "I hope you're enjoying the food."

Terra, with a mouth full of donut, gave her a thumbs up.

It was Kinzo who spoke up. Terra was proud of the story he made up, since elves weren't the best liars. "My uncle recommended this place."

Terina's brown eyes lit up. "Does he live local?"

"No, he came through the town on vacation and stopped in here for breakfast a couple years ago. He hasn't stopped talking about it."

"That's so wonderful. I'm glad he enjoyed. Word of mouth and my regulars is what keeps me in business." She winked.

Terra swallowed her bite and got in a word before Terina walked away. "Are you from here?"

"No. I grew up in Rhode Island, but my grandma lived here. I always loved the town and decided this is where I wanted to build a life and a business. I know the town is small, but the people are so nice."

"We're only passing through, but will recommend it to others. Do you have social media?" Terra asked.

Terina was elated and guided Terra to finding the shop on various social media sites. Terra ordered a few more donuts, and Meesha insisted on another meat pie, before they left. It was time to see Terina's home.

12

The small, three-bedroom, two-bath bungalow was as cozy in person as on the internet. Its simple gray siding, brick foundation, large front deck, and two car detached garage didn't say "a millionaire lives here". Inside was newly renovated and modern, with light wood flooring and plenty of windows.

The upstairs bedrooms sported slanted roofs and the light paint made them appear much larger than they actually were. From the moment they arrived at the simple country bungalow, Terra noted a shift in the energy. She was only beginning to get a handle on the various energies surrounding her and using them as a guide to paint a 3D image in her mind.

She should have brought a fae, since they had no way of entering the house without one. There was no key stuffed under a planter or over a door.

"I've got it!" Kinzo announced. "We can use the plants."

There were two planters hanging from the back windows with small herb gardens inside them. It was a brilliant idea. They could wake up the plants and speak to them, but the planters were too high even for Kinzo to reach. "How? We can't touch them." Terra asked.

Meesha glanced from Terra to Kinzo with a smirk. "Easy. You can't weigh much, I'll lift you up so you can touch the plants. Kinzo can take your hand and together you can send the message."

It could work. Meesha was a lycan — tall and all muscle. She bent down and Terra stepped onto her back. She was just tall enough to reach a low-hanging branch of one of the plants. Kinzo grabbed her other hand and together they thought: *Open the window.*

Nothing happened at first and she thought maybe it didn't work. A gust of wind blew across the tops of the trees surrounding the home and a leaf on the branch she touched wiggled, followed by a cascade of more leaves until the entire plant was moving as if stretching similar to what she'd witnessed in the woods surrounding the "dummy" Provence Academy in Lols.

"Is it working?" Meesha asked.

"I think so," Terra responded. The branches of the herbs slipped under the window and another gust from the trees swept beneath the small opening and slowly the window opened. "It's definitely working!"

Within a few minutes, the window had opened enough that Terra could pry it the rest of the way up and wiggle herself through it.

Meesha teased, "Great. You're heavier than I thought. That kiosk is putting on the kilograms."

Terra gave Meesha a sideways glance from the window. "Watch it! You can stay outside," Terra jested. She slipped inside, turning her back to the window. The room was exactly as her mind pictured it. She was making vast improvements with using her magical abilities, which she still didn't really understand.

Her brain and body buzzed as two energy sources competed for her attention; one was soothing like sage and the other vibrated like a bouncy ball. She closed her eyes, allowing the vibrations to spread through her body, then popped them open. The bouncy ball was above her head.

A knocking from the front door brought her out of her energy-induced trance.

She quickly ran to the front door and let Kinzo and Meesha inside.

"You check out the house. I'm going to take a look inside the garage," Kinzo stated. It was a detached garage, set between the trees.

Meesha took the downstairs and Terra headed upstairs, following the vibrations, a picture inside her head. As she climbed the stairs, the picture grew more detailed, and the energy inside the house… It was as if she could see the energy. That's what had been giving her images. The stairs led to a sitting room or game room. On one side was a large master bedroom. Two smaller bedrooms on the other.

She walked into what appeared to be an office. A laptop sat on a white desk with a view of the woods. There were built-in shelves on the wall filled with books. She thought back to her experience in Navarin and cautiously pulled a book from a shelf. She cringed, waiting for the house to fall apart, remembering the last books she grabbed that she shouldn't. When it didn't, she opened the book and glanced through it – recipes. For a bakery owner, that wasn't odd.

Placing it back on the shelf, she pulled a couple more books, finding more recipes. Taking out her phone, she snapped a few photos from the pages in the book then put the books back on the shelf where she'd found them. The bouncy ball vibration was closer than ever in the room near the built-in shelves.

Beside the shelves was a door. She pulled it open and entered a walk-in closet. On the bar hung various summer clothes. Sandals and dress shoes were stacked in shoe racks along the length of the floor to the bottom of the sundresses. *That's what she spent her money on,* Terra thought.

The energy smacked her as if the bouncy ball was ricocheting off her head. She slid the clothes back revealing a door. *A closet inside a closet?* She'd never seen or heard of such a thing. Without caution, she pushed the door open. It was empty. No clothes, shoes, or box clutter hidden away.

A rainbow of energy floated inside the room, and she recognized what she was seeing. It was a more detailed version of what she'd seen the night they mended the veils between the realms. This was a rift in the veil between Lols and somewhere else.

Terra noted the footfalls behind her as she swung around.

"Terra," Meesha called as she stepped into the room, scanning for Terra but not spotting her. "What... is that? What do you see?" Meesha asked.

Terra called from inside the closet's closet, "It's a veil to another realm."

Meesha followed her voice into the closet, a strange expression marring her features as she surveyed the closet inside a closet. She shrugged and unfolded her hand, revealing a clear plastic container with iridescent dust in it. "Navarin."

"Is that fairy dust?" asked Terra as she took the bottle, held it up, and stared at the sparkly material inside.

Meesha nodded. "I think so."

Both girls stared inside the closet. Terra seeing a rainbow of swirling energy and Meesha unable to see it.

Terra moved towards it. "I'm going in."

Meesha grabbed the back of her shirt, halting her. "Not yet, you're not. Let me get Kinzo and we'll make a body chain. We don't need to lose you on the other side."

Terra nodded in agreement to appease her friend, but she didn't have any fears about going beyond the veil, which she was now sure led to somewhere in Navarin. As she waited impatiently, she poked her hand through the veil. It was hit by humid air. With her other hand, she brought the bottle of dust closer to the veil. It jumped excitedly, giving her more reason to believe Navarin was on the other side.

Terra pulled her arm out as soon as she heard someone head upstairs. The footfalls on the wooden flooring were lighter than Kinzo or Meesha's, meaning a much smaller person. She closed the closet door and listened against it as the person paused in the middle room then walked into the master bedroom. A few minutes later, they crossed the middle room into the office.

She swallowed. Her options were limited. She could slip through the veil into what was probably Navarin, or wait for Terina or whoever was in the house to find her.

13

It was an easy decision. On the other side of the veil was a cave. The walls glittered with whatever was also in the bottle. Lavender, sparkling water washed onto a rounded shoreline at the edge of the cave and a small kayak was pulled up onto the narrow shoreline. It wasn't much to explore. There were no further tunnels. It wasn't more than a small area cut from the Seas. So Terina was fae, or part fae. *Did she know?* She had to know something. The kayak was a giveaway she'd explored at least some of Navarin.

Several minutes passed as Terra waited. She didn't want to head back through the veil if Terina was on the other side, but she had to get out of the house. After several more minutes, she got down on her hands and knees and poked her head through the veil. She figured if Terina was in the closet inside a closet she wouldn't notice her, being so low.

One glance showed the room was empty and the door still closed. She crawled further into the closet until the door opened. Her heart pounded as she slipped back into the cave and rested along the wall. She scrambled to the kayak and slipped into the lukewarm, sparkly water as she peered around the front. A foot, then a leg, followed by Terina, came through the veil.

Her eyes widened as she stayed as still as she could, keeping her eyes on Terina who immediately went to the wall and brushed something against it. Little sparkles fell into another small, plastic, transparent container. She did it with such care, Terra believed she did understand who she was or at least on some level.

Once the container was full, Terina headed back through the veil. It suddenly struck her: if there was a crack in the veil of rainbow colors in Terina's home, they hadn't truly mended the veils, or at least not all. Had no one strengthened the veil in Lols? After several minutes, she crawled out of the water and poked her head through the veil again. The closet was empty and the door closed.

She slipped through and listened. The eerie quiet of the house was broken by Meesha calling, "Terra! She's gone! Can you hear me?"

Her voice sounded to be coming from the back of the house by the window she'd opened and hadn't closed. Probably a good thing Terina hadn't noticed. She peeked her head through the window. "Catch me," she said as she scrambled out the window, trustbusting her friends to keep her from hitting the ground and breaking a bone.

"No... what are you—" Kinzo's words cut off as she dropped into his strong arms, hanging her arms over his neck in an awkward position. She couldn't help but notice his muscles and masculine scent.

She smiled as she glanced into his blue eyes. "You're a pal."

He let her feet down gently as she touched the ground, releasing her arms around his neck. She wondered what Nalysse might think if she'd seen them in such an awkward position.

She quickly wiped that out of her mind as Meesha urged, "Stop fooling around, we need to go."

Terra had parked the SUV further up the road, just in case, and was glad her paranoid adult-radar hadn't failed her. If they'd have parked in the driveway, Terina would have seen them.

On the way back to the hotel, she told them how Terina brushed the fairy dust from the cave walls, filling another bottle. The original bottle Meesha found stuffed into Terra's front pocket.

Once they reached the hotel, the others were waiting for them in the suite. Nalysse, Kayln, and Hyacinth were spread out on the sectional sofa, passing papers and discussing between them. Their discussion stopped as Terra, Kinzo, and Meesha came through the door. Terra placed the box of frosted donuts on the table. Meesha had eaten the second meat pie on the drive to Terina's. Terra, Kinzo, and Meesha joined the others.

Nalysse's eyes wide, her voice excited, and speech quick, describing how they'd found similarities in all twenty-one candidates. "They are all single, famous in their own right. It was Caspen who figured that out. Terina, she won the lottery. Samuels is a police chief who chases something called Big Foot. Another is a pro bono lawyer which Hyacinth said means he offers his services free. His services include wrongful death suits. Garney is a homeopathic doctor who specializes in herbal remedies. This one here," she held out a picture of an older woman in thick glasses, dressed in a business suit, with short salt and pepper hair trimmed neatly around her oval face, "is a college instructor who collects ancient artifacts."

Caspen strolled between Meesha and Terra's palms planted on the floor. "These are awesome," he mumbled, then stuffed the last bite of a frosted donut into his mouth.

Terra, Meesha, and Kinzo swapped glances, all thinking the same thing – fairy dust!

"What?" asked Hyacinth, noting the unspoken words.

"Terina is a fae hybrid. There's a veil in her house between Lols and Navarin. She goes there and collects… fairy dust."

Caspen swallowed his bite. "That's why these things are so good. I could eat several more."

Kayln put her arms around her chest defensively. "There's nothing wrong with fairy dust."

Caspen responded, getting what they were hinting at, "No, but what if she's putting it in the food? She knows what she's doing and…"

Kayln bit the inside of her lip. "She could be spelling the food." She deflated after admitting what everyone else was thinking. "But she wouldn't do it to hurt anyone," she snapped, in defense of a hybrid fae she'd never met.

Caspen shrugged. "I feel fine. A little full."

"You ate them all, didn't you?" Hyacinth asked with narrowed eyes.

He shrugged. "They were good."

Kayln squared her shoulders on a fae superiority trip. "You see! She spells them so more people will eat her food."

Terra thought back to her cream-filled donuts dusted with powder sugar. They were awesome, but she hadn't had any side effects from them unless — "Did we share a delusion?"

"No way," Meesha said. "Terina really came home. All that really happened." She glanced to Kinzo and Terra for support.

Terra pulled the bottle of dust out of her pocket and placed it on the table. "It really happened. She's spelling the pastries to sell more and keep herself in business. Here, places earn a living from what they sell. That's all she's doing. It's clever."

Kayln agreed.

"They are all aware of their magic. The lawyer who works on wrongful death suits, what do you bet he's a harvester? The professor who collects ancient artifacts is a troll, the police chief who chases big foot is a lycan," he continued, giving all twenty-one a possible connection to the realms.

The seven swapped glances. "There's only one way to know. We have to find all the veils that lead them to the realms."

14

An address popped onto the screen of Terra's phone. She and Tania had swapped numbers before Tania returned to Lols. Terra had texted her when they first arrived. Clyde hopped into her backpack. She lifted it onto her back and tiptoed across the floor so as not to wake anyone.

She was being selfish, but she was seventeen and hadn't seen Tania in a month. Every minute of nearly every day, she thought of her. Her golden-brown eyes filling her thoughts at night and the tender moments they shared as they discovered the realms together.

Her friends might be upset when they woke, but she had to see Tania before they went on their hunt for cracks in the veil or whatever it was they would find with the remaining twenty. A hand touched her shoulder and she stopped mid-stride, glancing over her shoulder.

"You're not going alone," Kinzo whispered, already dressed in jeans and a hoodie. His long hair draped over his shoulder.

Her smile dropped. "I'm fine. Stay here with the others."

He shook his head, indicating no, and reached his long arm around her, opening the door. She sighed. If she argued, it would wake the others. She stepped into the hallway, defeated, followed by Kinzo.

Once the door closed and they made it to the elevator, she spoke, "I'm going to see Tania. I'll be fine. You really should stay." Really, she wanted private time with her. That wouldn't happen with Kinzo there.

Kinzo pressed the L button on the elevator. "I know you're from Lols and miss Tania, but none of us should go anywhere alone. You chose us to come with you," he said in his serious voice.

She had Clyde, who was chittering in her ear as if he was scolding her. She pet his head. He was right, and so was Kinzo. She'd brought them all along. It wasn't safety in numbers she was concerned for, it was having her friends close, giving them a taste of her world. She nodded.

Two hours later, she was knocking on the door of a shared-room, gray brownstone with bay windows in Greenwich Village. The area bubbled in color and personality, reminding her a little of home. Tania's golden-brown eyes went straight to Terra as she opened the door, then drifted to Kinzo.

Dressed in jeans and a T-shirt, she was no frills, like Terra, which was another level they connected on. Her dark, shoulder-length hair was pulled to one side. "I didn't know anyone was coming." Tania said, trying to hide the disappointment in her voice, but Terra heard it.

Terra cringed. "He insisted."

"You know, I'm right here," Kinzo snapped, not enjoying being ignored.

Tania invited them in. The apartment was cozy. It was a studio. A single burgundy loveseat faced the bay window that overlooked the street. In one corner was a bed partitioned off with a bamboo dressing screen. A small kitchenette to the left of the entrance was sectioned off by a bar with two stools. Behind it was a couple cabinets, a few shelves filled with plates, bowls, and cookware. A sink, with a strainer beside it. On the other side was a hotplate and toaster oven. The refrigerator stood beneath the shelves. It was smaller than the one Terra had in her kiosk.

Terra felt awkward, as she'd wanted a private moment with Tania to feel her embrace and soft lips pressed against hers again. She had trouble focusing on anything else as they talked. Tania's gaze kept shifting to Terra, as if she felt the same. Clyde ran from one end of the small apartment to the next, crawling under furniture and climbing into small nooks and crannies.

Terra and Kinzo filled Tania in on what they'd discovered and, likewise, she talked about harvesting. She'd been provided a harvester instructor – Metford. The one who had been kicked off the tribunal for hiding her disappearance. Terra guessed it was his punishment.

He'd walked her through the process in his spirit form, but there were things Tania saw that the instructor didn't. "There's something I need to show you," Tania said, her words careful and deliberate. "It's not far, we can walk."

This piqued Terra's curiosity, and she was anxious to see what she was talking about. As they walked, Tania spoke, "The first thing I noticed was patterns. Some spirits repeat the same daily activities, as if trapped in a time warp, others appear and disappear. I thought it was because they were spirits, but even as spirits they are made of matter and energy. Then I realized it was something more. No spirit I've seen is acting in this dimension on purpose."

Kinzo gave Tania a sideways glance. "In this dimension?"

She shrugged. "That's what I call it. They are trapped, in a sense. Most don't realize they are dead. The ones on repeat are replicating their last day on Earth and dying over and over, others," she paused, "they move from one place to another instantly, as if searching for something. They can't see me the same as I see them, and they don't speak in words. I don't think they can."

Tania stopped walking and talking. Across the street was a cemetery. "This is cliché, but... spirits are drawn to cemeteries like bugs to a zapper. They appear and vanish, but always from the same location within a cemetery. Not like their headstone, but a literal location."

She strolled across the street. Kinzo and Terra followed as they walked past the open wrought iron gate and headstones, some new with flowers, other worn over time. She paused again. "Right there," she pointed. "That's the spot."

It didn't look like much, but with Terra's magic vision she saw a movement of rainbow-colored particles that danced in the air, similar to the veil at Terina's, but why would a veil be hanging out in a cemetery? "It's pretty. What is it?"

Kinzo lowered his brows and squinted his eyes, trying to see what they saw. "What do you see?"

"Colors dancing in the air," Terra responded. "It's beautiful."

"Hmm," Tania hummed, "I don't see colors. It's more like the air is shifting."

If hybrid magic worked differently, it made sense that they didn't see the same thing. Terra and Tania glanced at Kinzo and asked in unison, "What do you see?"

His shoulders drooped as if defeated. "Nothing."

Clyde jumped off Terra's shoulder and ran toward the colorful display. He sniffed around it, as if he understood they were talking about it. Terra wondered what he saw. He'd never been shielded by the curtains as he blindly ran through them, so maybe he saw the disturbance in some way too.

After a few sniffs, his tail went stiff, and he ran back to Terra. *What did you see?* she thought. As if he gave her an answer, she understood that he saw the colors too. Maybe it was her imagination, but she'd always felt she and Clyde had a psychic connection.

"You need to travel from place to place quickly. These disturbances are gateways from one place to another. They take me to wherever my mind says to go. Getting back is more difficult because I have to find another, but the spirits always lead me to them."

Terra wasn't able to see spirits, but she saw the gateway and felt its energy – smooth and steady.

"I call them elevators, because that's how they work. My thoughts tell them what floor to get off at."

"You think we can use them?" Terra asked, ideas of how they could use them bursting in her head.

"I don't know. You aren't harvester, but maybe."

Kinzo folded his arms over his chest in thought. "You're both hybrids, I'm not. I can't even see it."

Terra elbowed him in jest. "Stop being broody. There's only one way to know."

Tania winked and each hooked an arm around Kinzo.

"Where are we going?" Tania asked.

"Back to your place," Terra responded.

Kinzo pulled against them as they stepped forward. "I don't think I should go. What if my particles come undone, or I'm stuck in the elevator or other dimension or something...?" His voice drifted off as both girls gave him a 'you-have-no-choice' look.

"We'll superglue you together," Terra stated.

He lowered a brow in confusion. "Super glue?"

It always made her laugh inside when those in the realms didn't get the simplest human stuff. "It's strong glue we... Never mind. If it doesn't work and leaves you here, we'll come back for you."

Reluctantly, he gave in after they didn't give him much choice, and they stepped into the swirl of color.

A warmth enveloped them, and the colors joined together then dissipated as they stood, arms hooked together, in Tania's apartment. Kinzo wiggled his arms free and held them out for inspection as he checked to make sure all his body parts came through the elevator with him.

Now they had a method of travel. Kinzo stepped outside to wait in the SUV, giving Tania and Terra a moment together.

The awkwardness fled and the two stood by Tania's front door. It was if they were alone in the portable in Provence again. Terra laid a hand on Tania's smooth cheek. "I found the portal to Lols."

Tania folded her arms around Terra, bringing her closer. She tilted her head. "Where?"

Tania's warm, minty breath coaxed Terra. "Virgin—" she began to say, as Tania's lips crashed against her, swallowing the rest of the word.

15

"Where have you been?!" Nalysse asked in a sharp tone, lips pinched, and arms folded across her chest. She flashed Terra a hateful glance as Kinzo put an arm around her back to scoot her into another room for a private talk.

She held her ground. "No! I've been here worried while the two of you strutted around without waking us or saying a word to any of us, or me. You left without even saying goodbye!"

Terra recognized Nalysse's jealousy. It wasn't that on some level she hadn't considered it, and if she said she wasn't attracted to Kinzo she'd be lying. At the same time, she was far more interested in Tania, and Kinzo wasn't really her type. She was getting a sick pleasure out of watching the two argue, maybe because they were always so perfect. Elves were like that. They didn't even try, they just were.

Terra slipped away, joining the others, hoping they'd be more forgiving. Their faces mimicked Nalysse's. Hyacinth was still asleep, the door closed.

"She has a point. We've all been concerned. Nalysse was pacing. You could have left a note or something," Meesha pointed out, not hiding the disappointment in her tone. Of all her friends, they shared a special bond as magic tutor and pupil.

Terra defended herself, as if it would make her actions acceptable. "I tried to go alone, but Kinzo insisted on joining. I went to see Tania. We learned something new though." She hoped to refocus them on something other than Kinzo and Nalysse fighting and wash away any guilt she should feel.

The door slammed behind her, and her friends faces seemed to relax.

"Are they gone?" Terra mouthed.

Kayln nodded. "I think she's jealous."

Caspen sighed and shook his head. Kayln did make the most ridiculously obvious remarks.

Terra was a bit flattered that Nalysse would be jealous, and a bit annoyed. Kinzo was a straight shooter. He wasn't interested in Terra. A part of her felt bad, the other part felt flattered. She'd talk with Nalysse later when she was calmer. "They'll be back, but listen," Terra's voice excited. "We don't have to travel by car across the country." She started to explain all they'd learned while at Tania's.

Dark sunglasses over Bane's eyes, from behind the tinted windows of the vehicle he watched the teens from a distance. Keeping tabs on Terra in Lols proved to be more difficult than he thought, even with a taste of her blood. She'd discovered how to vanish and make her friends vanish with her. Nothing about the girl surprised him. She was resourceful. He'd figured out the disappearing act was some form of travel, but had never heard of such a thing, not even the all-powerful Cyrus could disappear right before someone's eyes. He pulled the fabric of the realms apart and stepped through or portalled, but didn't vanish.

The first time she'd done it was her little dalliance with her girlfriend and a male elf. He couldn't remember the young lady's name, nor did he care. His indiscretion was ancient history. The three were in a cemetery, then were gone.

He figured eventually they'd show up at the brownstone, since that's where they left the SUV. Sure enough, by the time he arrived, the elf was opening the car door and within a few minutes Terra had joined him. They went directly back to the hotel in Connecticut. Since then, they pulled the vanishing act each day. It made her difficult to track, as he'd find her location but, when he got there, she'd be gone again. They always returned to the hotel.

Early in the morning, they left then returned, taking the vampire with them. They'd vanished again. He used the opportunity to help himself to their room. The suite appeared as if seven teenagers inhabited it. Papers strewn about, clothes dropped in piles, and empty pizza boxes and soda cans. There was even a bakery box with remnants of telltale powdered sugar dried and crusted inside it.

He grabbed a printed paper off the table, holding it by the corner. The picture was of a college professor. Reading further, she collected artifacts. He chuckled as he read their notes. They were clever, as they'd discovered each had a special connection to the realms. Hybrids who practiced magic.

His job was Terra, nothing more. What they found or didn't find mattered not to him. She and her friends had discovered a mode of travel that had never been witnessed. A way of slipping through the realm undetected, not only Terra but her friends too. *What was she?*

Other than learning they were teenaged slobs, he discovered nothing useful. He'd learned more by watching the vampire sneak out at night undetected by the others. He planted a small listening device under a lamp in the living area and one in each bedroom. As a vampire, he had sensitive hearing, but the devices recorded as well, something he couldn't do.

Terra and her friends sat at a table sipping coffee at Byron Jones Community College, blending with the crowd. The coffee was crap. There wasn't enough sugar and creamer to make it taste good enough to actually drink, but it worked as a decoy. Nalysse and Kinzo were outside watching the instructor's car. Dr. Flaythem. The plan was they'd use their elf magic to talk with the trees, sending the message to Terra when the doctor left for the day so they could stealthily enter her office.

Realm Walker

She was divorced, older, no children or anything to go home to, and worked long hours. The class she taught ended at noon and now the sun was beginning to set. What was she doing all these hours? She'd left Clyde with Hyacinth at the hotel. Terra wasn't a patient person. It was Meesha who'd kept her from making a distraction so they could slip into her office. She said, 'She'll return if we do that and we don't want to hurry. We want time.'

Terra was about to burst, when a message was carried to her head. *She's gone.* Kayln did her fairy dust lock sigil and got them into the office. It was stacked with books, old books, new books, texts of all sorts.

Kayln went to the desk, while Meesha and Terra waded through the books. After sifting through a few, Terra found one of some interest. It was a journal that contained plans for an ascendent. It was a tool to travel to other realms. She tilted the book sideways and studied the drawing of something that looked like the gears of a pocket watch.

It had exact dimensions and worked by putting a special stone in the center when the moon was at a specific degree in the sky. It seemed pretty complicated to her. The stone looked more like a big golden seed. The author called it the heart stone. Whatever it was, it caught Terra's eye as something of interest and she snapped pictures of the pages with her phone.

"This might be of use," Kayln said, grabbing Meesha and Terra's attention as she dangled a key from a chain.

Meesha pushed the book off her lap and stood. "What does it open?"

Kayln beamed as she twisted the key chain in her hand and read the tag. "A room at Max Storage, Number 121."

Terra placed the book back on the pile, ready to vacate the dusty, messy office. "Let's go."

It wasn't difficult to find. An internet search showed there was only storage rental business in the area.

The unit was tidier than her office, and filled with antique treasures. Terra's eyes glassed over looking at so much stuff. She couldn't imagine why this woman had so much stuff. Was she a hoarder? A lonely woman with nothing to do but chase rare antiques?

Everything was in neatly arranged in rows. They each took a different row, not sure what they were looking for or even if there was anything they should be looking for.

There was jewelry and metal statues, even ancient coins, and an object that looked like an ancient twelve-sided dense metal helmet. *Ouch! What a headache,* she thought, imagining it on someone's head. She leaned closer, getting on her knees to study it. She'd seen pictures of them before. Her mind raced, trying to remember where she'd seen them. Then it came to her. In World History, her teacher had shown them pictures of the objects. He called them dodecahedrons. They'd been discovered in areas that were part of the Roman Empire. No one had been able to figure out what they were.

A scream interrupted Terra's thought, followed by a loud crash. She bolted to her feet and raced.

Kinzo stood by Nalysse's side, and Meesha walked around the corner the same time Terra did. Nalysse's eyes were wide as she pointed at a human-ish skull.

Kinzo opened his mouth to speak then closed it as Kayln rushed around the corner. A heavy gold crown embedded with an array of jewels on her head. Terra's attention shifted as did everyone else's.

"What's on your head?" Caspen asked.

"A fae crown," Kayln answered, matter of factly.

This caught everyone off guard as they forgot about the scream and the human-ish skull.

"How do you know that?"

Kayln smiled, satisfied to share that she knew something the others didn't. "It says so inside. King Rudino. We learned about him. His was kidnapped during the wars leading to the great war and neither him nor his crown ever resurfaced."

"Maybe that's him." Nalysse pointed, drawing attention back to the skull.

"Yuck," Kayln said, as she quickly took the crown off her head.

Without touching it, they studied it. Its surface smooth, the face longer than humans and its eye sockets more oval than round.

Caspen backed away from it. "I'm officially freaked out."

Nalysse seconded his thoughts as she stared at the objects she'd bumped into on the floor.

Terra scooted through the crowd. The aisles were narrower than grocery store ones. "I'll clean it up," she said as she bent down. "There's nothing here but weird artifacts. It's got to be the oddest mismatched collection of stuff anywhere in any realm."

"It's my mess. I'll help." Nalysse bent, lowering herself across from Terra.

The rest of the group exited and Kinzo waited by the door as a protective boyfriend. She guessed to appease Nalysse. He probably would have helped pick stuff up, but the aisle was barely large enough for the two of them on their knees.

Terra grabbed the last object, something that looked like a jeweled cross, but it was cyndrical with two cones on the sides that met in the middle of the cylinder. The stones each a different color. It vibrated in her hand as its energy moved through her. She placed it on the top shelf and followed Nalysse to the door.

Terra paused. "I'll be right there. I think I dropped my phone," she said, making up an excuse. The high energy vibrating object forced her attention. What other objects vibrated? She pressed her hand to the crown. It buzzed through her like a yippy dog. It was high energy, like the rock cross thing, and definitely fae.

She pressed her hand against the vibrating object again. It was warm, soft, and steady. Not like Lols, or any realm she'd been in. She looked closer at the cylinder. There was writing on it but, of course, it was written in a language she couldn't read. The other objects she picked up hadn't had an energy signature, why that one? Why the crown? They were imbued with magic, she thought, answering her own question. She snapped a picture with her phone.

She took one more glance around the storage unit. Where was the veil? There was always a veil.

"What are you doing?" Meesha asked from the doorway.

Terra turned and faced her friend. "Looking for a veil. There's always one."

Meesha twisted a long braid. "You're right. I'll bring everyone back."

"No, only I can see them. I'll catch up in a minute."

Meesha leaned against the door frame. "I'm staying right here. The veil could be one of those artifacts and zap you to another realm."

"You're a genius," Terra shouted as she looked closer at the artifacts, using her special vision. In the first row she'd been in, with the dodecahedron, was a tall, narrow metal thing with a door. Colors of light shone through the crack of the closed door.

She raced to the tall metal object. "There." She pointed.

Meesha wrinkled her nose. "Looks like a torture chamber."

Terra thrust the door open. The colors swirled inside. "I'm going in."

"At least it's empty. No skeletons of tortured lycans or vampires awaiting rebirth." Meesha grabbed her hand as Terra crawled into it and vanished through the veil.

16

Fast food and milkshakes in the hands of the teens as they returned to their room. The day had been more of the same. Sure, they'd found some interesting and creepy stuff but, like all the rest, Dr. Flaythem was a hybrid connected to the realms. The veil in the tall metal object took her to Verboten, as expected.

Clyde ran beneath Terra's feet, excited for her return. She reached down and rubbed his head. He moved a paw over his head, playing with Terra's hand.

Hyacinth grabbed a blood bag out of the drawer she'd stuffed them in and poked a straw into the top.

"All this seems too convenient," Caspen stated, after swallowing a bite of a veggie roll.

His thoughts mimicked Terra's. It all seemed more than convenient, like someone had already done the research and sent them on a wild goose chase.

Kayln picked at a salad with her fork. "Are you saying they wanted us out of Provence? But why?"

Caspen shook his head. "That's not what I said."

"They aren't really interested in bringing in five new tribunal members from Lols," Nalysse said with a bite to her voice. She avoided any eye contact and stared into her salad.

Terra knew Nalysse's comment was meant to hurt her. She was still bitter about Kinzo leaving with her to visit Tania. She sucked on her chocolate milkshake. She was more interested in the moment and enjoying unhealthy fast food.

"We've wasted four days. What do we do now?" Kinzo asked, all eyes diverted to Terra.

Everything they'd learned pointed to the tribunal members, or someone, researching before even sending them. *Who? Did she even care?* Each one had magic of sorts and a ticket to another realm. Some of the veils were mended, but not all. The homeopathic doctor's remedies sounded very similar to elfin remedies. She put her shake on the table and took the list out of her pocket, crumpled it, and threw it like a basketball towards the trash can. It hit the edge and dropped to the floor.

She didn't care. If what they were doing was purposeless then she'd do what she really wanted. "We're done," Terra announced. "I have a better idea. We leave tomorrow."

Chasing the teen was a thankless job and Bane was limited during the day. He pulled off his scarf, sunglasses, hat, and jacket, tossing them on the back of the hunter green chair and sat on the matching love seat in his room.

He took a sip of microwaved blood from the cheap hotel disposable cup. He preferred a warm meal. The job of the tribunal was to come up with solutions when something spilled over from one realm to the next. A vampire in Canida fit, but if he were still on the tribunal he'd have suggested they send qualified adults to Lols to investigate. Not a group of teens.

He tuned his vampire hearing toward their conversation. A smirk crossed his face. They figured it out. The whole thing was a witch hunt, but it took them four days to figure it out. Now they were planning on leaving again. Great! No ideas where to. Luckily, he'd taken the opportunity, when he had the chance, to taste Terra's blood and could follow her anywhere.

Lifting his legs, he propped his feet on the footrest and tuned them out, his senses gravitating to what was happening around them. He jumped from the sofa and pulled back the curtain. His vampire senses picking up two people outside the hotel creeping around.

In a teal flash he portalled to the alley between the hotel and Rico's Mexican Cantina and Grill. Spices filled the air that no longer teased his taste buds. There was a single light in the alley that spread over a figure. A male; his long, dark hair falling over his back. Bane walked silently towards him and wrapped his arms around the man's chest and arms, tightening so he couldn't get free. "What are you doing?"

A sharp pain burned into his leg. He glanced down, noting something that made him look closer. A lightning beam in the shape of a sword stuck out of his leg from the man's palm. He tightened his grip and the lightning sword vanished. The man choked, trying to catch his breath as strangled mumbles left his mouth. Something sharp burned across the back of Bane's legs. He twisted around, keeping the man in front of him. A woman glared at him with threatening eyes.

"Let him go," she ordered, a whip of blue light spinning in the air like a lasso from her hand. Her blonde hair in a high ponytail, she was dressed in black leather with knee-high matching boots.

Bane laughed. "You're cliché." He didn't know what they were, nor had he ever seen anything like the blue light whip she created from the palm of her hand. As a three-hundred-year-old immortal vampire, he didn't fear them either.

She stepped closer, her light whip circling right to left. A few strands of Bane's hair lifted and relaxed from the shift in air as the whip came increasingly closer on either side of him. He would not be intimidated by her. Bane squeezed the man harder, drawing his last breath out of him, then reached a hand through the man's chest and pulled out his heart. Blood dripped from his hand as he opened his arms, the man's lifeless body puddling to the ground.

Anger marred her almost beautiful features as she thrust the blue whip at him, wrapping it around his body, cutting the fine threads of his suit. Anger pushed its way through him, overcoming any pain he might have felt. She'd ruined his suit! Her feeble whip couldn't hurt him, as he would heal.

He dropped the heart and vanished in a teal light, portalling behind her. Wrapping his hands around her neck, he squeezed.

A high-pitched scream pounded against his ear drums, pain shooting through his head, as he dropped to his knees, hands over his ears.

The sound subsided and she was gone. Unsteadily, he climbed back onto his feet and glanced at his suit. Burn marks from the electric whip cut through the fine expensive threads, exposing his burned flesh underneath.

In his long vampire life, he'd never seen a creature that could create plasma whips and knives. He studied the man, then collected his heart and licked a drop of blood from it. Concentrating on the tangy taste, he couldn't place it. A hybrid maybe. He couldn't be sure. Taking a microcontainer, he filled it with the man's blood.

17

Terra's eyes filled with water as the elevator took them right into the bottom story of her childhood home. Her best friend, Noah, on the couch waiting. "Noah." She ran the few feet between them and nearly tackled him. He folded her into his arms and squeezed. "You dropped off the grid."

She squeezed him back. "I did." Tears streamed her face. She pulled back and wiped them.

He brushed a hand across her cheek, pushing stray hairs from her face. "It's only been a month."

"It's felt like forever. You won't believe everything I have to tell you."

"You can start with your new friends," he jested, pulling her in for another hug.

In her excitement, she'd totally forgotten she'd brought everyone with her. She introduced everyone and they retired to her dad's office.

It was time she discovered what her dad knew. Emotions overwhelmed her as she studied his desk. Her mind pictured him sitting in his thick, comfy, ergonomic computer chair with a mug of coffee. He'd lean back and take a sip, then pull himself forward and plug away on the computer again.

She ran a finger along one of the large computer screens then the next. Closing her eyes, she took a deep breath and turned to face her friends.

They were chattering quietly. Kinzo by the window, staring towards the hill and Coit Tower, Nalysse standing beside him, their hands entwined. Hyacinth and Meesha were on the leather sofa and Kayln was studying the titles of the array of computer books. She tucked a short hair behind her ear.

The bottle of her father's cognac on the desk where they'd left it the night she and Noah spent drinking before she was sent to live in Provence. For a moment, she lost herself in the memory. After a glass of cognac, he switched to beer like her, and they reminisced about her father until they fell asleep.

That was the night before she learned she was going to live with the aunt she'd never met. She shuddered at the memory. She stayed with Noah and his mom after her father passed, and a social worker came by. Thinking back, was it really a social worker or someone sent by the tribunal? She wouldn't put it past them, although he seemed pretty human now that she remembered him.

She grabbed an empty glass from the bar embedded in the bookshelves and poured the smooth, dark liquid into it. "I think you need some before I tell you more," she said, handing Noah a glass of the smooth cognac. He'd need it to process what she was about to tell him.

He took the glass and swirled the liquid. "This is big. Bigger than living with a mysterious aunt in a shelter off the grid?" he asked, running his free hand through his now purple hair.

She nodded. "much bigger."

Her friends' eyes silently agreeing with her.

He studied everyone's face then took a swallow, then a larger one as he sat in one of her father's plush brown leather chairs. "I'm ready."

There was so much to tell him. She barely knew where to start, but figured the beginning would be the best place. "My aunt lives in a place called Provence City. It's like living in a snow globe, without the snow, located squarely between seven realms…"

Half-way through, he poured himself more cognac and studied her friends. Not once did he look shocked or surprised. Rosette hadn't told her much, but Kinzo had and it boggled her mind. Noah stayed calm and cool; maybe it was the cognac. When she was finished, he leaned into the plush back of the chair and nodded. "That explains why my phone calls dropped. I couldn't even leave a voice message."

That was it. He was in shock. "Noah, we are all from different realms. Realms. Not countries, but realms with magic and…"

"Remember that book we found?"

What? That caught her off guard, then she remembered. They'd found a book titled in a handwritten word: 'The Origin'.

"I read it. It's all about those realms."

Terra grabbed his shoulders. He blinked his eyes as if waking from a dream. "We need to find five people here that can serve on the tribunal, and I know you can help." He was also an expert computer nerd like her father.

Clyde jumped onto the desk and reached his front paws on Noah's chest as if to beg.

Noah picked Clyde up, who pulled himself onto his shoulder and nuzzled his neck. "OK. I'm in."

She didn't think it would take much convincing, but was really shocked at how nonchalant he was about the realms. Granted, it did take a lot to get him worked up. Like her father, he was a computer nerd. His skills would be invaluable.

Terra missed the sunlight as it spread over her shoulders and head as Meesha guided her in a magic lesson. The energy of Lols was like a heartbeat. She used her vision to allow the energy to paint a picture in her mind, still unsure what else she could do with that. Meesha wasn't sure either.

"What do you see?" Meesha asked.

"A map divided into equal grids; waves move through it like ripples in water."

The door opened. Terra and Meesha turned to Noah.

He pushed his hands into his pockets. "I set up a search algorithm that will find the identifying characteristics you asked for."

Terra motioned for him to join them. "Remember how we used to play out here while my dad barbequed?"

"I do. That night before you left…" He paused. "The book we found."

She nodded. Meesha stood. "Keep working on it. I think the ripples might be sound waves." She rocked on her feet. "I'm going to raid your kitchen."

Once the door closed, he let out a breath, as if what he had to say was difficult or mind-boggling. "I read it. At first, I thought it was a fantastic story but now, after everything you told me today, I don't think it was. Your dad knew about everything."

That was exactly what she thought. It was the only answer that made sense. Thinking back to their last Christmas, when her father had given her the tiara, was there something in the gesture or did he simply want to share a piece of her mother with her? He could have shown her the book instead. Had he left her clues? The night they found the book they'd passed out and it became a forgotten memory. "Do you have it?"

"It's in your father's office, where I found it."

Suddenly, it dawned on her, something else she remembered from the time after her father's death to the time she was sent to Provence City. The weird guy they followed that ordered two coffees, same time, same day, every week at Noah's boyfriend Jakob's workplace.

They'd followed him to the main library, where he vanished into thin air. "That guy we followed to the library. He knew about the elevators." She grew more excited as she talked about it and her mind pieced it together. "The two coffees he ordered, but only drank one. He was probably a Harvester hybrid, and the extra coffee was for the dead person he met every week. Tania says some spirits repeat the day of their death, day after day. They don't know they are dead."

Now that she said it, she felt bad they followed the guy. His story was heartbreaking, but so was hers. At the time, she was grieving her father and following the guy was a distraction.

"The elevators are how you travel from one place to another… Is that how all seven of you appeared in the living room yesterday?" Noah asked, still processing everything.

"Exactly. They are located various places and will take you wherever you want, but you have to find one. I bet the main library has one. I couldn't see it then, but I've been in seven realms now. Every one I enter, my ability to harness magic gets stronger. We have to go!" She jumped up from the wooden patio chair.

"What about the book?"

She shrugged. "I'll look at it later. The library will close soon."

18

She put Clyde on his harness and told the others they were going for a walk. It wasn't a complete lie. They'd walk to the bus stop, get off a few stops later, and walk to the library.

Clyde bounced as if pleased to be home. She left him in front of the library with Noah since animals weren't allowed and would surely catch someone's attention. In the middle of the library, where she'd witnessed the man disappear, was the familiar disturbance, exactly as she thought. Colors glowed and swirled in the familiar rainbow pattern. The man walked into it, vanishing before her eyes. This expedition, more than anything, confirmed what happened in her mind.

It also proved others knew about the elevators and who knew what else. A chill crept up her spine. Those in the realms thought they were hidden, better than those in Lols, but commoners, or humans, had found ways to harness magic.

Its energy smooth, she cleared her mind and stepped in. Matter swirled around her, and she felt as if she could grab and mold it. She pressed her fingers into the colorful swirls. They parted and her hand went through. Since discovering them, she had used them for transport not study. Now she looked with a different eye.

She couldn't touch the molecules around her. They followed her hands as she circled them in front of her face like a psychedelic trip. Drawing an air flower, then a curved line over it, for a moment it looked like a rainbow over her tiny flower until the molecules, always in motion, erased it, reminding her of Oobleck.

Returning to Noah, her mouth ran wild as they walked back to the bus stop. "It's there, like I thought. I stood in it instead of traveling and was able to mold it then it would melt away. It's wild. I think it's part of how I control magic, but I don't really understand yet how. I walk through curtains, see veils and maps in my head, now I control matter that others can't even see."

"Slow down. You're a hybrid, right?"

REALM WALKER

His statement reminded her of Cat. How she read the first page of the book written in old fae. As the words fell from her mouth 'Follow the path of the footsteps' she hadn't been able to read further as the ground under their feet shook like it was pulling apart. It was a magic Cat didn't know she had.

Bjorn was also a hybrid ice dragon/air fae. He didn't have much dragon, but enough he spat frozen ice pellets instead of sea water.

Hybrids used magic in ways purebloods couldn't. She knew that, but it finally really sunk in. Her power to manipulate magic was only developing and, based on what she just did, she could mold… energy. "I guess." She wasn't so sure anymore what she was.

By the next day, Noah's algorithm had found two young people; a kid named Alex who was clairvoyant, and a girl named Kenya who called herself a witch. Alex didn't live far away, the other side of the bay in Santa Clara, but Kenya lived in Minnesota. Terra was the only one who could see an elevator and she was in charge. It was her team and her realm.

The Land of Lost Souls

She figured Nalysse wouldn't like her choice and cringed slightly. The tension between the two lessening instead of snapping like a rubber band. The mission was more important, and Kinzo made a good team player, so she took him and Kayln. If she was going to meet a witch, she needed a fae, and an elf was a good idea since, together, they had enough power to wake the plants.

She could have chosen Caspen, or even Nalysse, but at the moment she didn't trust Nalysse and she had other plans for Caspen. She sent him, Nalysse, who practically hissed at her, and Meesha, who'd keep Nalysse in line, with Noah to Santa Clara.

They used the elevator at the main library. Clyde climbed into her backpack, which she left open a couple inches for air. The library was the closest one she knew of. One minute they were staring at the massive inside of the structure, and the next wishing they'd brought jackets. Fall in Minnesota was colder than she thought, but the colors of the trees were magnificent. The leaves red, orange, and yellow. It was similar to the colors in Connecticut. Lols had its own beauty. Each realm seemed cut from a piece of Lols cloth.

Kenya twirled a lock of her dark hair, and her friend popped a bubble. She wondered how Noah was faring with Alex.

"What are you smoking?" Kenya finally asked. Her sarcasm smacking Terra in the face. She probably would have said the same thing a few weeks ago.

She was fae alright. They were… snooty and entitled. Kenya had a curiosity about her but even so seemed a bit overwhelmed. "We can show you."

Kenya's dark eyes studied their faces as she twisted a ring on her left hand.

Kayln wiggled her fingers over her warm coffee and whispered something Terra couldn't hear. The coffee instantly bubbled into a gas that Kayln blew towards the girls across the table from her.

They watched in curiosity, then folded their arms around their middles in indignation.

"How did you do that?" Kenya's friend asked, the red hair on her arms, matching the red hair on her head, stood at attention.

"The same way you spell the jewelry you're wearing," Kayln noted as the girl clutched the jumble of bangles on her arm.

Terra wasn't sure how Kayln would ever know such a thing, but it wasn't the first time Kayln surprised her. The girl's eyebrows lowered in concern.

Kinzo touched the wilting daisies in the center of the table and their leaves stretched and the flower spread its petals towards the light.

Kenya mumbled something and her spoon lifted from her thick vanilla shake, danced above it for a minute, before dropping into it. "So, you're like us and we're supposed to believe you and what… congratulate you or something?"

Definitely fae, definitely fae. Stay calm, you've survived Halsey. "You have time to think about it. I'll send you a meeting time beneath the old bridge." That's where the elevator was. She assumed the girls would bite. They'd found each other, surely they were curious about magic.

Terra was a straight shooter and laid it out for them. She guessed the friend was at least part troll. As Kayln had pointed out, the jewelry, probably the ring Kenya kept twisting, was spelled like the bangles on her friend's arm. Noah's search formula found her frequenting a witch site online.

By the time they returned to San Francisco, Noah and the others were there. They talked over pizza. A three meat for Meesha and Noah, veggie and pineapple for the elves, and pepperoni for her and Kayln.

Hyacinth was buried in Terra's computer in the guest room. She didn't join them for dinner. She liked her blood bags chilled and Terra kept them in the back of the fridge.

"Alex is more than clairvoyant. He sees colors in words," Noah said, grabbing the large slice of pizza with both hands.

"That's how he knew we were telling the truth."

Kayln harrumphed. "We had to show Kenya and the other girl... what was her name?"

"Warlita," Kinzo responded.

"That's it. We had to show them," she said in annoyance.

Terra held in her laugh. Dealing with fae was always like that. She was convinced, simply by her attitude, that Kenya was at least part fae.

Alex was blind, except the colors of words, and he needed DNA to see events. Terra thought that was cool. She hadn't really figured out her powers yet, which spun her attention back to Kayln. "How did you know Warlita had powers too?"

Kayln chuckled. "Easy She's troll. You can tell by all the bangles on her wrists, rings on her fingers, and homemade earrings. Trolls are smiths and miners of precious metals and gemstones."

Not every troll was studded with jewelry like Warlita. In fact, most of them wore little jewelry. It was their colorful tail plumage and short stature that gave them away. She did have very red hair. Did she have a tail? Terra couldn't help but wonder.

The Land of Lost Souls

Noah dusted his hands and wiggled the mouse on the computer.

Since they found Warlita too, they only needed one more person if she could talk Mario, the bobcat shifter they found outside the Lols side of Provence Academy, into it. He'd be number four. That was tomorrow. The day after they went back… and with them, they'd bring the five hybrids.

Noah swallowed his bite of pizza. "We have choices. Dena is eighteen, she's been researching the power of suggestion, and Payton, he's in a couple online Wiccan groups."

They already had a witch. The power of suggestion was different. What subspecies hybrid could possibly twist things with language? "Dena."

Most of the group stayed at Terra's house. She took Meesha and Kayln with her, leaving Nalysse with Kinzo. She'd given her such nasty looks the previous day she was afraid she'd turned into a jack-o-lantern ready to snip off her nose.

Dena, a pudgy blonde, was friendly and bubbly. She seemed very receptive and almost relieved to talk to others who had odd abilities. Somehow, these teens had awoken magic in Lols. She doubted any of them understood how, but it also seemed the longer they were in Lols the more alive everything became. It's energy a rhythmic heartbeat that fluttered in excitement.

Dena's powers were more than the power of suggestion; she communicated with insects. Terra remembered something from her second magic lesson with Meesha. She'd said something about elves communicating with insects and small animals. So far, she'd only seen elves communicate with plants. Was it a twisted elfin skill that only some, or hybrid, elves were able to do?

"I wish I could learn that," Meesha said, as they watched leaves rise into the air and spin, insects jumping from one leaf to the next like acrobats. Dena was like the Snow White of bugs.

She gave her the same instructions. Now it was time to find Mario. He was the reason she'd brought Meesha.

Mario wasn't difficult to find. They already knew where he lived, and Meesha's sensitive nose tracked them to a high school where he was in soccer practice.

Meesha swallowed a bite of cheeseburger, followed by a drink of orange soda. Terra was amused how easily they'd adapted to human, *commoner*, food. "He's pretty good. It's his extra ability that gives him the speed," she noted as they watched from the bleachers.

His agility was a cut above everyone else. Terra swallowed the fries in her mouth. "You think he'll want to leave this?"

Meesha shrugged. "I don't know. The side we saw that night was scared. I think he's still scared and would be willing. In Provence, he'll learn to control magic, not let it control him. It's hard. As a wolf, I retain myself, but I'm an animal and animal instincts can take over if not trained. I don't think he has any control over shifting either. That's something I can teach him."

She took another drink. "How are you doing?"

There were things she hadn't told Meesha. "It's different. I can see the elevators. The other day, I stepped into one and stayed. Matter of all colors swirled around me and when I moved my hands it followed. It seemed I should be able to mold it somehow…" Her voice drifted off. She had no idea what to do with her skills. They seemed useless.

"You're a hybrid, maybe you can."

That was the problem with being a hybrid. She could access magic, but hadn't a clue what to do with it. All the kids they'd met, even the hybrids in Lols, learned to manipulate their magic. Hers gave her 3D images and helped her see portals, veils, curtains, and elevators. What was she supposed to do with that?

"Looks like practice is over," Meesha stated as she stood, stuffing the last bite of burger into her mouth and crumpling the bag.

They waited outside the locker room until he came out; hair wet, it fell to his shoulders in waves.

He joined them. "I saw you on the bleachers." He rocked on his heels as he spoke, as if nervous. "I didn't think I'd ever see you again after that night. I even convinced myself that night wasn't real."

It hadn't been that long ago, just a couple weeks.

Meesha nodded. "That's the change. It tricks your mind at first."

That was the other reason she'd brought Meesha along. They were both shifters. Terra followed behind, listening to their discussion as they walked.

Meesha reassured him: "It's rough at first until you learn to control it. Once you do, it becomes easier."

"There's no one to teach me." Mario stopped and turned towards Meesha. "I know it gives me abilities other people don't have, but I'm afraid I'll hurt someone."

Meesha laid a hand on his shoulder. "I can help you; we can help you." She pointed to Terra. "Not everyone where we live can change like you and me, but they have other abilities. I think you'd benefit, and I could teach you. We have a whole school that could help teach you. Right now, we need willing participants to go there and show that commoners like you count. You matter."

He met Meesha's gaze then Terra's. "What is her power?"

That wasn't an easy answer, nor did she know how to show him. "I see images in my head, like I can see the floorplan of a building without walking inside it." That gave her an idea. She focused her energy toward the school building. Its halls and rooms becoming visible in her mind. She described them to him.

His eyes narrowed. "It's a public school. You've been inside it."

Why did she need to prove anything to him? About 200 yards away was a home in the woods they were cutting through. "That house. It's a private residence. Inside the back door is a TV room, to the right is a hallway that goes to three bedrooms. There's a bathroom between two of the bedrooms. It doesn't have a tub, only a shower. The third bedroom has a large bathroom with a separate tub and shower. To the left of the TV room is a kitchen and a door that leads downstairs to the finished basement. It has a ping pong table, and the walls are painted in chalkboard paint.

His mouth dropped and his eyes widened. "You see all that?!"

"I'm right."

He nodded. "Yeah, that's my neighbor's house. I've been in there many times."

"Do you believe me?"

He nodded and glanced at the fallen leaves on the ground. "It wasn't that I didn't believe you. I… this whole thing, my changing and becoming something else, it's all crazy and I'm scared."

Terra knew that feeling too well. She sympathized with him, but he'd never learn control if he didn't come with them. "I get that more than you know. A couple months ago, I was a normal teen entering her senior year then my… father passed away and I had to go live with my aunt and everything is weird. I want my old life back. I want to go across the street and visit my best friend. You have a choice. You can choose to come, or you can choose to stay. I'll contact you when its time and you can meet me at the old building where we met the first time."

He shook his head. "I should be going. Mom will have dinner ready, and… thanks." He managed a smile.

The sun dropping low in the sky, it was time for them to return to San Francisco.

19

Terra found herself surprised as the words tumbled from Hyacinth's mouth. "I think I found the vampire bit by a lycan." She completely changed the topic as she sat down on the floor, holding her knees to her chest.

Terra had nearly forgotten about that terrifying experience. She and Tania went into the lycan realm of Canida, and were hunted by a vampire in its big cat form, when a lycan in its wolf form came out of nowhere and attacked it. She and Tania rolled out of the realm, literally, and into Provence where level 3 hardcore magic wasn't allowed, or even possible. Of course Hyacinth knew. Everyone in Provence knew, even if they didn't speak of it and, with Devan on the tribunal now, she wondered how many secrets Hyacinth was privy to.

Hyacinth continued, her voice sad and a little nervous, as if she felt guilty, "In Drakonia, we haven't lost one of our own. The only other place a vampire could come from is Lols."

Silence fell over the group.

"What else?" asked Terra, the wheels in her head spinning, but not connecting. There was something to Hyacinth's discovery, but she couldn't quite grasp it.

Hyacinth continued explaining: "It's much bigger than a vampire accidently falling through a veil. There are clans here…" She paused, her eyes connecting with each one of the group. "They stick mostly to themselves, and I don't think they know anything about Drakonia or the other realms. There's an entire night world that lives under the cover of darkness and hides in the shadows."

The other side of the story was werewolves. Real, and here in Lols. They live in packs. She figured they came in centuries ago and those werewolves were a hybrid form of lycan. Their bite, though, can be fatal to a vampire if not tended to right away.

There were a lot of implications in her words. If there were vampires and werewolves here, then there had to be strife between them. One blaming the other. They were natural enemies.

Caspen grabbed Hyacinth's hand and brought it under his chin. "You've been leaving at night."

She nodded, almost in shame. "When I wake up during the day, you're all gone so I've been on the computer, in chat rooms, and that led me to the Lols battle between werewolves and vampires. I've left a couple nights and I think I found her. We have a lycan, three and a half elves, and a fae. I think we can help her."

"She's a cat like you. You learned to control yourself in that form, she hasn't, and so you want to help. Your heart is gold, but we can't walk into a vampire clan and ruffle things up," Caspen said, his fingers sliding gently over her hand. That was the prey in him.

Hyacinth, though, as a predator, didn't feel the same fear. They didn't have the same cunning or caution.

Caspen was so loving and gentle. Terra's own heart longed for Tania, but that wasn't happening. She refocused her mind. "She's right. We need to do something. There has to be something. We can't ignore this." She stared at the pureblooded elves, lycan, and Kayln. That was probably the predator in her showing its face.

"Like what? I can't spell it away with fairy dust," Kayln stated, her voice indignant.

"We should do something good before we go. The least we can do is try to save a life before we go home!" Terra said, her tone more forceful than she intended.

The room fell silent.

After several minutes, Nalysse twisted her hands in her lap. "I know a recipe, but I don't know the plants here," she stated, interrupting the silence.

Their eyes spoke what no one wanted to say out loud. There was no cure. Kinzo tilted his head, his ponytail falling over the chair. "How do you know it will work?"

"I don't."

"How do we know she's even alive? We'll be stepping into a battle with those older and stronger than all of us," Meesha stated.

No doubt they could be stepping on a hornet's nest, so to speak, but Terra couldn't not at least try. "Maybe we aren't as old or strong, but we can't leave the vampire without at least trying." Her words spurred with a tiny bit of guilt. It was her and Tania the vampire was after.

After hours of research, they found herbs in Lols that contained similar healing properties. A trip to the local nursery, they collected the herbs needed, and a trip to the grocery to collect the tools.

Nalysse, using her comicay, recalled her grandmother's recipe. She was a little girl, about 6, maybe 7. It was a two-part remedy that included a salve for the bite and a drinkable formula.

Laying the herbs on the table, Nalysse assigned each jobs that included grinding, cutting, stirring, and smashing various parts of the plants. Included was an unspoken tension over whether it would work or not, since the herbs weren't exact, and it was speculation that there was a cure. It was always said there was no cure for a lycan bite to a vampire.

Nalysse turned off the burner on the oven and blew out a breath as she sat on the couch.

Kayln stood above the salve and hot formula and sprinkled something into them.

The actions didn't escape Nalysse's eyes as she jumped up from the couch. "What are you doing?" she shouted, as she ran to towards the table.

Kayln huffed. "No formula is complete without fairy dust."

"This is an elf formula. It doesn't require your dust. You may have just ruined all our work. There isn't time to make a second batch." Fire burned in Nalysse's eyes and words.

Kayln rolled her eyes. "The dust will accentuate the healing properties."

Nalysse rolled her hands into fists by her side as she channeled her anger.

Hyacinth interrupted. "I think everyone needs sleep. It's been a long day." She was the only one that'd had any sleep. "I'll wake you when it's time."

"Terra," Caspen's voice cleared through the fuzziness of her sleep. She popped her eyes open.

Worry creased his eyes and marred his face. "Hyacinth left without us. The formula didn't work. The vampire is worse and they are holding her in a room," his voice trembling.

Terra sat up abruptly, pulling her legs over the bed.

Kayln, lying next to her, stretched then popped an eye open. As if reading their expressions, she opened the other and sat up. "What?"

"We need to wake everyone. Hyacinth left without us. We have to get her," Caspen said in a shaky voice.

Within minutes, the three of them woke everyone else. "She's in Vermont. We have less than three hours until the sun rises there. We have to go now!" Terra urged. They scurried out the door and ran to the closest cemetery. The library was closed and out of the question, but she remembered Tania said ghosts are attracted to them and often the elevators can be found in cemeteries.

Hyacinth wore her comicay, which is how she communicated with Caspen. At least they had that. She wouldn't have worn hers, which made her rethink their importance. Sure, the tribunal or whoever could pull up their memories and probably track them, but if Hyacinth hadn't had hers, they wouldn't know where to begin.

With no real plan, the elevator vanished, leaving them across the street from a two-story brick home. A single streetlight at the end of the cul-de-sac illuminated the average, but large, home with a gate made from thick metal bars around it, and trees.

The neighborhood was rural but had other homes within walking distance. Terra used her vision to paint a picture for every one of the interior rooms of the house. Downstairs was a kitchen with a back door and living room, bathroom, dining room absent of a table. Instead, it had a wraparound bar and padded barstools. Behind the bar were two refrigerators. She shuddered, realizing they were probably filled with blood. Upstairs were five bedrooms and three baths.

"There's five and Hyacinth. She's upstairs," Meesha said as she sniffed at the air.

Kayln pulled her arms around her middle to keep in the warmth then wiggled her nose and twisted her mouth. "I think I can open the gate." She rubbed her hands together as if they produced fairy dust.

"No," Kinzo said, his breath steaming in the chilly air, stopping her before she tossed fairy dust on the lock. "We shouldn't all go busting through the front gate."

He was right. Meesha was the only predator with them. They couldn't use brute force.

"It's a good distraction," Meesha offered. All eyes drifted to her as she laid out a plan that included Clyde. Terra was a bit nervous about it. She hated using Clyde, but it was a solid plan and he was small enough to go through the bars of the gate. Terra, Nalysse, and Kinzo would cause a commotion which would draw the vampires out. Terra would go in and rescue Clyde. While that was happening, Meesha, Kayln, and Caspen would sneak over the high gate, into the house.

Terra pressed the button on the gate. A disembodied, aggravated voice came through a speaker. "Can I help you?"

"My ferret went through the bars of your gate," Terra said in conjured tears, real caution prickling her spine.

"Wait there," said the aggravated, disembodied voice.

A few minutes later, a couple of vampires appeared. One a short woman with golden hair, dressed in tight pants and a long-sleeved tee. Walking with her, the other vampire was a thick male. His dark, curly hair cropped short, and dark skin was a contrast to the female.

"I'm so sorry to wake you, but my ferret," Terra sobbed, hoping her nervousness was hidden under her sadness.

The vampires stopped short of the gate, annoyance painted on their faces as the female pressed a button.

The gate slid behind the tall fence. "It's your ferret?" asked the male, giving Terra the eye.

She nodded, rubbing her sleeve beneath her nose as she sniffled. "He ran that way." She pointed towards a grouping of bushes in the opposite direction from Caspen, Meesha, and Kayln.

The vampires glanced at each other then Terra, Kinzo, and Nalysse. "You can come in ,but your friends can't," the female said with annoyance.

Kinzo stepped beside Terra and folded her hand in his. "He answers to both of us. Can I come in with my girlfriend?" Terra felt daggers from Nalysse's eyes stabbing her back.

The female vampire narrowed her eyes as she studied him and Terra. "What are you doing out at 3:30 am?"

Great! Of course, it was a natural question. Three teenagers taking a stroll by their home in the early morning wearing PJs. Not a single one of them in a coat.

"We went for a walk," Kinzo said.

He was becoming an expert liar. She was rubbing off on him. She squeezed his hand.

The male vampire studied them up and down. "In your pajamas?" he asked with skepticism.

"Yes. I caught my boyfriend cheating and needed the support," Nalysse spat with fire in her voice.

"Fine, you stay here," the female said with no expression as she pointed at Nalysse. Terra couldn't tell if they believed the story or not, but caught the jealousy in Nalysse's words.

Once Terra and Kinzo stepped through the gate, the female vamp pressed the button and the gate closed, leaving Nalysse outside it.

Sudden chills ran down Terra's spine. *Clyde*, she said mentally.

"He went that way," Kinzo said, turning to walk towards the grouping of bushes.

The Land of Lost Souls

Caspen dropped inside the fence behind the house joining Kayln after Meesha hoisted them over.

"There're still two vampires in the house. You and Caspen go inside and hide while I distract them."

Kayln's brows furrowed. "What are you going to do?"

"What lycans do. If they haven't caught my scent yet they will when I shift, and I'll make sure they see me. "Go!" Meesha urged, pulling a shoe off her foot.

Kayln sprinkled fairy dust on the lock, drew a circle around it and blew, then whispered the old fae words. The door unlocked, Caspen opened it and they went in. Kayln gently closed the door. Moonbeams and flashes of light from the TV gave them enough to see. They quietly padded to the entryway between the kitchen and dining room, their hearts beating so loud they feared the vampires would hear them. Caspen peeked his head around the corner into the dining room.

He let out a quiet breath of relief when the room was empty. The stairs were to the right. He pointed for Kayln to get behind the bar then followed her when she was safely hidden. They lowered themselves, their backs against the thick wooden frame.

Footfalls pushed against the floor and the light came on then moved into the kitchen. "What are you doing?" asked a female voice from the living room.

"They're here," responded a male.

"Who?"

"The werewolves. They sent the vampire and now they are here for us."

"You're probably smelling the neighbor's dog. He doesn't like you," the female vampire jested.

"It's mutual and, no, I'm not smelling the dog. It's muskier, like the vampire. It stank like it's been hanging around with a pack that lives in the woods."

The female harumphed. "Vampires don't work for werewolves."

"That one does." His voice becoming more forceful. "Get off the couch!"

"Fine. We'll go on your witch hunt." The female vampire chuckled. "You stay ahead of me. They can bite you first."

Once the vampires left, Kayln and Caspen ran for the stairs, their heartrates up. Neither Meesha nor Terra were sure which room Hyacinth was in. Caspen tried the doors on one side and Kayln on the other. They didn't have any time to waste. Doors flung open as each raced down the hallway.

"Hyacinth," Caspen called as he came to a locked door.

"Caspen," Hyacinth responded, her voice strained. "You're here. Get me out."

"She's here!" he called.

Kayln joined him and, using her magic, opened the door. Moonlight spread over the chair in the middle of the room; the curtain wide open. Hyacinth's head rose as they entered.

Caspen went directly to her side, folding his arms around her. "I'm here."

Kayln studied the ropes holding her wrists and ankles, and noted the burn marks on Hyacinth's skin. Vampires didn't spell things like fae; they had strength, speed, and exemplary senses, but not fairy dust and spells.

"Can you untie me?"

Caspen reached for the ropes.

"Wait." Kayln put up a finger to stop him. "The ropes are spelled."

"They burned at first. Can you unspell them?" Hyacinth's voice reached a high octave, aware the sun would be peering over the horizon soon.

There wasn't an option; but was the spell fae, troll, or elf? She didn't have time. She was a fourth year spellcasting student who'd learned old fae as a second language. *I can do this. Think. Druppo is a simple fae sigil that wouldn't work on something spelled by elves or trolls.*

There was only one thing that burned vampires – UV. She'd never heard of a spell that coated something in it. She needed something heavy. Kayln whispered as she blew dust from her hand on the ropes and massaged them, crossing her fingers metaphorically. They dropped, falling to the floor. Kayln sighed relief. Caspen took Hyacinth in his arms.

"I'm sorry I did this on my own," Hyacinth whispered, wrapping her arms around Caspen's neck.

The moment was sweet, but they needed to get out before they were discovered.

"No time. We have to go," Kayln said with a sense of urgency, interrupting the lovers' moment. She wasn't one to normally butt in but wanted out of the house.

"The girl." Hyacinth turned her head and pointed towards a bed neither Caspen nor Kayln had noted in their rush to save Hyacinth.

On the bed lay a vampire. The covers pulled to her chin, all that showed was her swollen face covered in black spider lines.

"We can't. There's nothing we can do. We tried," Caspen pleaded as Hyacinth kneeled by the girl's bed.

She pressed her hands on the edge of the mattress. "I'm so sorry. I wanted to help you. I did. I thought the elf potion would work." Her voice cracked as tears dropped from her eyes.

Kayln put an arm around her. "We tried. We did, but we have to go before they come back."

Hyacinth wiped her eyes and nodded as she rose to her feet.

Caspen wrapped an arm around Hyacinth, as her ankles were in bad shape from the ropes, and helped her downstairs and to the back door. Kayln pushed it open and the three ran for the fence line. Hyacinth's wounds healing with each painful step.

We have her, Caspen's voice said into Terra's mind through the comicay.

Clyde put on the act of the night, as he'd stayed hidden in the bushes surrounding a large tree in the yard. The show was over, and it was time to collect him "There you are," she said as she picked up Clyde and bundled him in her arms. As if he understood her telepathic 'stay still' message, he didn't squirm.

Kinzo put an arm around her back as he steered her toward the exit, hoping to get out quick. "Thanks, we got him."

The vamp lady stood in front of the gate. "That," she said in disgust, eying the furry ferret in Terra's arms.

That. Terra's blood boiled and she spoke before she thought. "That is my ferret and best friend."

Kinzo nudged her, urging her to be quiet. He was right. Her emotions got the best of her at times.

"Yes, that. It looks like a monster rat." The male vampire sneered.

Terra took a deep breath. Heat rushed into her cheeks. Biting her tongue wasn't an easy task. She knew she shouldn't irritate them, but wanted so much to punch them in the face.

"Don't let them out," came a male voice from the direction of the house.

Great! Great! Had someone checked on Hyacinth? They were busted.

The male vamp narrowed his eyes at Terra and Kinzo then turned and met the other one. The female glared at them from the gate.

Terra tuned in her still developing predator hearing as the two male vamps spoke.

"There was a wolf. We chased it into the trees, and it vanished in a portal, and the vampire is gone."

A blue light flashed in the woods behind the house, followed by another soon after. The sky was clear except for stars and a sliver of moon. That ruled out lightning. The blue was a teal shade. The veils; were they ripping in front of her? She didn't feel a shift in the energy. She refocused her mind on the vampires, letting the blue flashes simmer in the back of her mind.

Both male vampires who'd joined the female shifted their gazes to Terra and Kinzo. "You think those two had something to do with it?"

Of course we did! These vampires were idiots. Terra had always been good at thinking on her feet. Why couldn't she think of something now. She turned to the female vampire. "We really should go. My parents will be worried if they get up for work and I'm not home."

The female pressed a hand on her jutted hip, clearly annoyed. A blue light flashed outside the fence, catching Terra's attention. The vampire didn't take notice. Another one, perplexed she couldn't figure out the blue flashes.

The female straightened her legs and pressed her hands behind her back. "You aren't going anywhere."

Great! Terra searched the other side of the gate for Nalysse. *A little help please,* she thought. "We really need to get home."

A male vampire folded his arms over his chest. "Where is she?"

Kinzo swallowed. Terra felt his nerves as he wrapped an arm around her shoulder. He stumbled over his words, "Him… We have him. We'll be out of your hair—"

A flash of teal enveloped her and Kinzo. Its warmth gathered them, and Terra finally got it as the light faded. A portal. They were standing on the fourth floor of Provence Academy.

"You're lucky I got you in time," Devan said in his adorable Australian accent as he walked to the side of them.

Terra would have felt eased and safe, except her aunt and a few other tribunal members stood in a circle around them. Their faces a symphony of anger, frustration, and worry.

Fantastic! They were in deep trouble.

20

Lupe, Meesha's mom and a tribunal member, narrowed her eyes, focusing on her daughter then shifting her gaze to the rest of the group. "Lycan bites are lethal to vampires. What were you thinking?"

Terra shifted uneasily. "We—"

Hyacinth cut her off. "The wounded vampire. I found her. I thought we could help and…"

"Help! Of course! Now you've made things worse. The vampire isn't healing, is she? This is why Lols is a prison realm." Mina, Kinzo's mother and eldest elf, spat, her eyes narrow and fixed on her son.

Prison realm? It wasn't a prison. It was her home. Terra felt heat rise in her cheeks. The words that rolled from her mouth were meant to sting. "Lols is my home! You banish hybrids there. Anything that's happened is your fault because you are the ones who can't handle hybrids who have access to magic different, and sometimes more powerful, than your own. This whole mission was bogus!"

Rosette's pursed elfin lips unpursed as she spoke. "What are you talking about?"

"The list. It was a bogus list. You already knew all those people...*commoners*," she spat, stressing the word, "have magical abilities and access to rips in the veil. You didn't actually plan on bringing five commoners to the tribunal." Terra folded her arms across her chest in defiance.

The tribunal members glanced at each other, dumbfounded, then Allwyn, Kayln's father, cleared his throat. "We don't appreciate your tone or innuendos. We had every intention of bringing in five commoners."

Terra rolled her eyes. "Five commoners you chose! Not an election, nothing done in fairness."

"Where is the list?" Rosette asked, her bat wings larger on the shadow on the wall.

"In the hotel trash where it belongs," Terra huffed. She had five ready to come at her say so. She glanced to Hyacinth who wobbled in Caspen's arms.

"You were only to watch, not interact. Now we have to fix this. We will bring your actions to the tribunal tomorrow. Now go to your rooms. Tomorrow, you return to classes and don't speak a word," Lupe said, her voice stern enough for even Terra to consider whether to defy the tribunal.

Hyacinth stepped forward, her legs wobbly. "I did as you asked. Don't put this on them."

The parents looked to each other, guilt in their faces. What Hyacinth said was true. Terra couldn't believe it. How could they? How could Hyacinth? She felt betrayed. "That was the purpose of the mission!"

Allwyn took a deep breath as his eyes went from the other parents to the group, focusing on Terra. "That was a small part. We don't always approve of tribunal decisions, but we must respect them as diplomats."

Seriously? How could they stand there and make them feel miserable when they wanted the vampire found? They tricked them! Heat rose to Terra's cheeks as expletives yearned for her mouth to release.

"She wasn't to engage. None of you should have engaged," Lupe said as she glanced at her daughter. "What you did was dangerous."

How dare she try and put the blame on them? Terra's lid exploded. "You sent seven teenagers. What did you expect us to do? When was the last time we listened to any of you?!"

Rosette's face flushed with Terra's words. "We expected you to listen," she said as her voice shook.

Terra flashed a glance at Rosette. She couldn't tell if the trembles in her voice was down to anger or embarrassment. It didn't matter to Terra. They were the adults.

Bane looked at the young vampire from Lols. Her face puffed like a chipmunk from swollen glands and black veins. There was no cure for a lycan bite. The girl would surely die.

If it wasn't for the drop of Terra's blood he'd tasted without M'ra's permission, he wouldn't have known where to find the vampire. He'd taken the blood the night he snuck into her room to count the passports on her chest. Luckily, he did and, with even more luck, they'd distracted the vampires enough he was able to go in and grab the girl without being noticed.

He was sure the tribunal would be concerned about that, ask questions, even watch the teens' comicay footage, but they wouldn't find her.

His comicay vibrated against his arm. He depressed the middle and a holograph popped up. No one had seen M'ra in centuries, not even those with high authority or who, like him, reported directly to her. A sense of privilege overcame him as he took in her fine features, shaded hair, and dark olive skin. She didn't wear the veil. Did that mean she trusted him?

Remorse drew her lips together as her hazel eyes fell upon the girl. "Did you recover the serum and salve they used?"

"I did. I've sent it to the lab."

"Blood samples too?" she inquired.

He nodded. He didn't expect the young vampire's condition to affect him as much as it did. He'd seen death, but hadn't witnessed the likes of a lycan bite until now.

Without taking her eyes off the girl she asked, "What else did you learn of these commoner vampires?"

"They live in groups and are mortal enemies with werewolves. I assume those are hybrid lycans. Unfortunately, she was bit by a true lycan. She may have survived a werewolf bite."

"It is our kind that decide the fate of vampires, choosing to give them the option of a second life. That is our way. We don't decide. We only give those a second life that are dying in the first and qualify for the privilege. These vampires aren't following our ways. How are they deciding who gets to choose? How are they turning them? I need to know who is responsible. Go back to Lols. we need blood samples to trace parentage."

She was right. Somehow these vampires had found a way to create new vampires and he had a new job. He glanced back at the girl. "Is this always how it looks?"

"It is. She doesn't have long." With a tilt to her head, she glanced at Bane. "Can you get a sample of Terra's blood?"

He knew better than to ask questions. Her blood was a direct route to understanding her hybrid ancestry, but the tone in her voice teased at something else. "I'll do that tonight as she sleeps." He wasn't a taster, never had the ability to trace heritage through blood, but he knew when the drop of her blood touched his tongue that she was something different.

"Tell no one and send it directly to me."

"There's one more thing."

She raised her brows. "Go ahead."

"In Lols there were people sneaking around the hotel. I killed one." He noted her frown of disapproval. "I didn't have a choice. They were different. From their palms, they had plasma that took the form of a whip and a sword. It burned like sunlight. One got away, but I tasted the other. It was tangy and affected me."

"A pureblood?"

He didn't know, but hybrid and commoner blood didn't make him feel tipsy. "I think so. I took a sample and sent it to the tasters."

"You'll let me know what they discover."

"Yes, of course."

She faded and the call ended.

M'ra wasn't exactly what he expected. Over the many years, his mind had formed an image of her and now he had to rewrite that image. Whatever was happening was covert. She could have easily spoken through someone by channeling, or wore the veil as she usually did, but she chose to show her face to him. *What did she know?*

Clyde in Terra's arms, she placed him on the floor as she unlocked the door. She was so angry she didn't notice Halsey wasn't there. Clyde jumped onto her bed and ran down the length of her legs, tucking his head beneath the covers, then twisted his body and peeked at her from beneath the covers. Then he scurried up her legs, resting against her chest. The tribunal called a meeting for the following day, giving the parents time to brief the rest of the tribunal. To her, it was like awaiting sentencing.

She smoothed her straight, short hair back against the pillow and stared at the ceiling. "They are horrible." She ran her hand along the top of Clyde's head. He nudged her chin then jumped from her bed to Halsey's.

As restless as Clyde, she couldn't stay locked in her room awaiting punishment. Maybe they'd send her back to Lols and she could put everything behind her.

She sat up. "You need fresh air."

Clyde ran to her feet and followed her out the door. She didn't bother with his harness. At least they hadn't posted anyone to guard her.

When she passed Hyacinth's room, she paused. The door wasn't closed all the way. She pushed it open. Kayln and Hyacinth were sitting in the middle of the floor cross legged. Their heads turned toward Terra. "I came to see how you were feeling."

Without responding, Hyacinth urged, "Come in and close the door." Her tone carrying a 'this-is-top-secret' tone.

Terra always liked to be in on the good stuff which incidentally followed her around.

The Land of Lost Souls

The fuzzy pink area rug was soft as she sat. Fur going through her hands as she rested on them.

Hyacinth showed her wrists. "They're almost healed." She paused and sucked in a breath. "Only UV rays burn a vampire, and they take longer to heal."

Kayln pushed a few lavender strands of hair falling in front of her face and surprised Terra with her words. It wasn't like Kayln to say something smart. "I'm in L4 spellcasting and have been taught old fae and spells since I was born, I think. There are no spells that use UV light, not fae, not elf, not troll."

What did that even mean? Terra had nothing. She didn't know a thing about spell casting, except what she'd learned from the fae around her. Elfin spells worked different. It was the combination of herbs and ingredients that made elfin remedies work and she hadn't yet learned about how they used fabrics and yarn.

Hyacinth pressed her comicay. "It's better to show you."

Terra's heart clinched as she saw Hyacinth bound in a chair. The female and one of the male vamps that had been outside were with her. An older, staunch man with salt and pepper hair came into the scene. The edges of the memory were fuzzy, so she couldn't tell if he'd already been in the room or entered through a door. Her hands behind her back he walked to them, and lightning beamed from his hands as he said something that sounded a lot like old fae. He moved to the front and did it again.

She'd never seen anything like it and, from the expression on Kayln's face, neither had she. "What did he say?"

"'Infuse', that would be the old fae interpretation and, since the ropes continued to burn her, I think it's a low level sigil that infused UV into the threads of the rope."

Terra's eyes moved to the fading burn marks on Hyacinth's ankles. "I'm sorry. How bad did it hurt?"

"A lot and I heard it fizzling like electricity. It burned worse at first and lessened. I thought..." She paused. "I thought I was going to meet the final death, then the light went away and they left me in the room."

They exchanged similar expressions, then Hyacinth explained how she thought maybe the guy was some kind of hybrid, since magic worked different for them, but she had no explanation for how he knew old fae; neither did Kayln.

Terra remembered the pictures she'd taken in Lols at the creepy artifact collector's office and the object that buzzed with energy. She pulled out her phone and handed it to Kayln.

Kayln's face twisted as she studied the pictures. "The first is an ascendant and the other I'm not sure. It says 'inside is hidden, unlock and find'."

Of course, it didn't make sense, but it made her more determined. If there were things in Lols that dangerous it was more reason to bring in five tribunal diplomats to smooth the way for Lols inhabitants to become part of the realms. It was offensive not defensive. Growing up, all she knew about magic was what she saw on TV. Was Lols gaining magic or was she finally seeing it? She didn't have an answer. "I'm going back," she stated.

Hyacinth's eyes met Terra's. "No! I tried doing it alone. I'm sorry. I shouldn't have. Look at me. These burns should have healed instantly but the marks are still there, reminding me how foolish I was."

"You made that decision but it's the tribunals fault. They asked you to find her."

Her eyes dropped as she stared at the fuzzy pink rug. "I made a deal they wouldn't wipe our minds…" Her words trailed off.

Kayln planted her arms on her sides and blew out her already round cheeks. "That wasn't a good deal. We all figured the whole mission was bogus…" She studied her friends' faces. "You didn't?"

Kayln was back. Her moment of intelligence was foreshadowed by a silly response.

Terra ignored Kayln's comment and said to Hyacinth, "If you had told us, we could have done it together, but what happened, happened. We are all fine and I'm going by myself. You're all in enough trouble. I'll be there and back. All I'm doing is collecting them. I'll even leave my comicay on just in case."

Hyacinth pulled her eyes away from the rug. Her expression one of understanding, "Then you need to know everything I learned about the night world."

21

The Tribunal

Elin, the newest harvester on the tribunal, as she took Metford's place, spoke with a 'let-me-get-this-straight' voice: "The vampire had the location of the commoner-vampire and didn't report it to us. She told her friends?"

Maglesh, the third troll, stood. "If they knew her location, why didn't they report it to us? They were told not to interact?" His yellow plumage pointed towards Devan as if to blame him.

Devan was Hyacinth's brother. He wasn't going to let anything happen to his sister, so had kept tabs on them and in communication with her. "Hyacinth has a huge heart and I'm sure they thought they could help her. I warned you this could backfire."

Lupe, who generally remained quiet, but this involved her daughter, stood. "A lycan bite is death to a vampire. There is no cure. Why would they think there was one?" Her glare focused on the elves.

"This isn't a blame game. They are teens. When was the last time your children didn't take risks?" Ernessa, the uptight vampire who had no real ball in the game, seethed. She thought it was stupid from the start to trust a group of teenagers with tribunal business, especially the female vampire. "Did they at least accomplish anything? The list, where is it?"

Lukas, a lycan who wasn't fond of the testy vampire, replied, "A team was sent and found it crumpled in the trash at the hotel. All their belongings have been collected and brought to the school."

"Where is the vampire?" asked Maglesh. His plumage twirling in the air.

The eldest vampire stood. "It's a female. The team was unable to recover her. She is gone."

Colton, the fire dragon, his hair as red and hot as the flames teasing the back of his throat, roared, "Gone! What do you mean 'gone'?!"

Devan, the youngest member of the tribunal, was angered and repelled by the way they were acting. They were adults in charge of making decisions for the realms and they couldn't even have an adult conversation. Hyacinth was his sister and she'd been in real trouble. "As in not there. Someone moved her."

A fae stood. "I think we need to see their footage."

The dean's voice interrupted Rosette's thoughts: *Terra hasn't shown to class and isn't in her room.* That was great! The testy teen was causing her a huge headache. If she didn't tell the tribunal, she'd be kicked off just like Bane and Metford, and if she told them the consequence would be losing Terra. She'd surely be banished back to Lols. She needed her here, especially if what she said about the veils in Lols was accurate. It meant they didn't mend them all. The spell wasn't powerful enough. They needed her. She cleared her throat. "The veils in Lols; some are weak and ripped." She proceeded with extreme caution so as not to alert them to Terra's true nature. Hybrids had unmapped skills so it was possible… "Terra can see them."

The members of the tribunal stopped arguing and all eyes focused on Rosette. Not what she wanted. "We can use her and the potion to find the weak spots and mend them, but I think she's gone back, as the dean can't find her anywhere." Her voice trailed off as she cringed mentally at the backlash.

The repercussions Rosette expected didn't happen. No one cared if she could see the veils or not. They were worried about their own hides, or at least the troll was.

"Her mind was bent right?" asked a female troll with orange tail plumage. That was just like trolls. They missed the ocean for the lake.

"Not exactly. It was a rescue mission. I don't have the ability to wipe minds," Devan stated.

Terra collected the group, meeting them at the elevators. Each in awe of how she could see them and more surprised at how they could travel by using them. It took only an instant to get from one to the next. The final stop was the Lols side of Provence Academy, where Mario would be waiting.

Missing her classes surely brought attention and might mean her own banishment, but they'd asked her opinion, sent her on a mission, given Hyacinth a private mission which almost cost her life. She had five willing commoners. They waited in the woods until the rustle of leaves told them someone was coming.

Mario's dark, curly head appeared behind the half-naked trees as he climbed the hill. "I've never skipped school. It felt good to get a bathroom pass and not return," he said, facing the group. A wooden block in his hand.

He noted Terra's eyes on the block. "I don't need that," he said nervously. "Bathroom pass." He dropped the wooden block.

Terra did quick introductions. "I don't know what we're going to face when we get to the fourth floor. It might be empty, or the dean may be waiting. Even worse, the tribunal might be waiting but, whatever happens, you belong there as much as anyone. Remember that."

She took in a deep breath as she turned the knob to the fake Provence Academy. Waves of trepidation from the group filled her. She felt their nerves and imagined their sweaty palms as they marched up the stairs. When they reached the door to the fourth floor, she turned and faced the group. "This is it. There are stairs on the other side of the door. Once we go up them, we cross the curtain and enter Provence. If anyone wants out, say your piece now."

REALM WALKER

Kenya stepped forward and held up a hand. "I'm in. Who's with me?"

The others glanced to each other then Kenya and pressed their hands together.

Terra opened the door, not knowing what awaited them, and led the group up the steps.

22

Warlocks

Hidden in the trees, a young blonde woman with a high ponytail and knee-high leather boots and a young man, long, dark braids falling over his shoulders, watched from a safe distance as Terra and the group of mismatched teens entered the old, worndown building.

"That's her," the woman said.

The young man listened to the forest; cracking leaves as small animals walked over them, the sway of the branches as the wind pushed them, and anything that sounded out of place. The fate of Juwel's last partner wasn't pleasant, as his heart had been torn from his chest by a powerful vampire. "Should we go in?"

"Give it another minute or so."

The warlock council chose him for the mission. He had no choice but to go. The briefing short, he understood the teen girl with short multi-colored hair was special. He felt her energy. It trailed and beamed from her. It wasn't like anything he'd ever seen. She'd bounced onto the warlock radar when she came in contact with an object his people had spent centuries searching for.

At the time, she was with a different group of teens than she was with now. Juwel and her last partner were unable to be sure which teen woke the object. It was further unclear as they all traveled through the mysterious elevators. He saw her clearly, which was most likely why he'd been chosen. He had an impeccable ability to see and hear energy.

Juwel pushed the nearly naked branches. "Now."

Hank walked through the opening and turned when a voice brought his attention front and center.

"Why are you following her?" said a mid-height man, a scarf around his face, a hat on his head, dark glasses over his eyes, and designer jeans and boots.

Juwel threw lightning rods at him and missed, as the man vanished and reappeared behind her, knocking her into the dirt.

Hank backed away. He should fight. No, she was older and had far more gifts than he did. If she couldn't save herself, what could he do? *Die, like her last partner.*

"What is your interest?" she seethed, palms pressed against the leaf clutter on the ground.

He pressed a designer boot against her back. "I asked you first."

Hank cringed. He had no choice. If he didn't at least try, and she survived, he'd never live it down. He'd be ridiculed and tortured. He pushed a lightning rod toward the vampire's face and pulled the scarf.

The vampire caught the edge of the scarf with his hands and spun around on his boot, digging it further into Juwel's back. He pressed his boot down, smashing her to the ground. "Clever. What do you want with her?"

"We… uh… she…" Hank stumbled over his words as a lightning whip moved behind the vampire, close but not touching, until it formed the shape of a sword and cut through his back.

He couldn't see through the scarf but imagined the vampire's face wasn't expressing agony but anger, as he pressed his boot further into Juwel's back. The lightning sword fizzled as he ground her into the dirt with so much force blood pooled from her body.

Hank took the moment the vampire was distracted to run.

The familiar shift in energy caught Terra as she stepped onto the fourth floor.

Rosette and several other adults she recognized from the tribunal stared at her. Steam seemed to radiate off Rosette's head, but that could have been smoke from the red-headed fire dragon behind her.

"You were told to go to your room and to go to classes," Rosette growled.

Terra held her hand up behind her back for the others to stop. They hadn't reached the top of the stairs yet. "I did go to my room yesterday. You," she studied all their faces, "sent me on a mission. I accomplished it. You said to choose five. I chose five, but not from your list. We chose our own five." She motioned for the others to come up the steps. She took a couple steps forward to make room.

"We didn't ask you to kidnap five children," a lycan roared.

"I didn't kidnap them," she bit back in defense. They weren't small children. "They are here willingly. They have magic because there's magic in Lols, but you all knew that. You didn't think we'd figure it out. Level three magic, even. The hard stuff!" she said in defiance.

The dragon behind Rosette spoke, "We should send them back, all of them, including Terra." He pressed a large hand on Rosette's shoulder.

Terra took his gesture as a threat to Rosette, and she was suddenly moved. "Take your hand off her. This had nothing to do with her. The tribunal sent me, not Rosette. You will not banish her or kick her off the tribunal unless you're all willing to make that sacrifice."

He dropped his hand, not in fear but guilt. It was written on his face as his eyes dropped.

"She's right. We sent her and didn't specify she had to choose from our list. We also used Devan to send his sister on a private mission to find the vampire. They are teenagers, what did you expect them to do? It's our fault. It's all our fault, and Devan took the risk and brought them home safely," the new harvester, Elin, said.

Hyacinth was on a different mission. She hadn't said anything to them. This hurt Terra, but they also learned something new about hybrids in Lols. Not that she any had idea what it meant. Lols had other problems too, like the weak veils.

Mario stepped forward. "I want to learn to control the animal inside me. Every day I live my life afraid I'll turn and lose control and… hurt someone."

Kenya took his shaking hand and stepped forward. "My emotions rule my curses. I once hated a girl so much at a softball game I wished the ball to hit her in the face. It left the bat and curved directly towards her, hitting her square in the nose. She hit the ground so hard it gave her a concussion and the ball's contact broke her nose."

Dena stepped forward, taking Mario's other hand. "I found my words have power when my sister and I had an argument. I told her to jump overboard, and she did – off the roof. Luckily, we had a trampoline beneath."

The dragon raised his hand. "I suppose you all have such stories to share. We don't need to hear more. You will be escorted to an empty house under guard until the tribunal decides what to do."

Terra let out a long sigh, followed by biting words, "Under guard? They aren't a danger. You're the ones who wanted representatives for Lols. Well, here they are. Normally, each realm gets to decide who represents them. Lols wasn't given an opportunity. I found a group to represent Lols' interests and you're going to keep them under guard!"

"For now, yes. We will meet with the tribunal and, over the next week, we will interview and speak with them. Once we've decided their future here, we will reconvene."

"It's not up to you. I represent Lols and Lols needs a voice. They can go to the academy and learn about the realms and how to work and control their magic," Terra demanded. How dare they think it was their decision alone?

"I don't mind them questioning us," Dena said quietly. "It's kind of a lot and I'd like to ask them questions."

Warlita and Mario seconded her statement. Terra glanced at the group. "We should discuss it."

The tribunal agreed to give them time to discuss. They drew back to the stairs, out of sight of the tribunal.

"Would you rather go to the school or stay at a guarded house under scrutiny?" Terra asked.

"I'm OK staying at the house for a few days as they sort things, but we shouldn't be under guard. We haven't done anything wrong," Kenya said.

Of course, there was nowhere for them to go either. They didn't know Provence or where to find the realms they might be able to enter.

The others agreed. It was a lot for them, and they hoped to do things more diplomatically. No guards, but they'd stay at the house and answer questions so long as they could ask questions. The tribunal agreed.

The five were led down the stairs by a lycan sent by the dean. Terra turned to follow them when Colton stopped her. "Not you. This doesn't involve them, but we have questions for you."

Terra paused on the step, let out a frustrated breath, and turned. Clyde scampered behind her and laid on the floor in front of her feet.

Ernessa stepped through the crowd of members. "The team sent to Lols didn't recover the vampire. She wasn't one of ours. Drakonia's concern is others are sneaking into our realms through cracks in the veil than the opposite would also be true. Did you see weakened veils when you were there?"

The vampire narrowed her eyes, but her voice, besides being annoying, didn't elicit real concern. Terra didn't like her and maybe that's all it was. No, it was more. There was something she wasn't saying. Terra had the idea she'd know what it was soon. "I did. In several locations."

The diplomats searched her as if trying to decide if she was telling the truth then Maglesh, the outspoken troll who stood in the front, spoke but not to Terra. He turned his attention to a young fae. "How long will it take for the fae to make more potion to seal the veils in Lols?"

The young fae, Olivia, spoke. Her voice quiet. "Not long. A few days, but we will need more limestone and hemlock."

Judge, whose voice was loud naturally, asked, "How do we know it's not the potion causing the veils in Lols to weaken?"

Olivia shifted on her feet but didn't speak. Liam, the eldest fae, moved front and center as if to save the timid fae from further questioning. "Are your veils weak? Has anyone else entered your realm since we strengthened them? I say we put it to a vote here and now!"

Tired of standing, Terra dropped to the floor and played with Clyde. She wanted to leave, but figured she'd gain and learn more by staying. When the count was done, 29 voted for strengthening the veils in Lols and 6 voted against.

It was decided this would be done. Adult teams from each realm would be chosen to go to Lols and mend the veils. Once the potion was made, a date would be chosen.

23

The teal sky darkened as she took her seat at their patio table. It was the first time they'd all been together in the portable since Devan brought them back. Terra wasn't the first, or the last, to arrive. She sat in her usual seat at the table. Everyone in their normal spots as Kinzo and Nalysse trailed in a few moments after her.

Hyacinth reflected on the previous night. Desperate, they'd been willing to entertain her remedy and left the patient to the final decision. In her weakened state, she agreed. She applied the salve first around the bite. The cells and tissue around the bite black and flaking as they were dying their final death. She then drank the oral serum with help. The vampires around her so loving and caring as they lifted her up and held her, another tipping the serum into her mouth.

At first, there was no reaction, then blackness crept through her veins at a quickening speed and her lymph nodes started to bulge. Hyacinth was nearly in tears reflecting on the story. "I thought, if anything, it wouldn't make her worse."

Nalysse dropped her gaze to the table; in guilt or sorrow, Terra couldn't tell. "You tried. We all did," Terra said to comfort her friend.

"I know. I was so hopeful it would work." She sighed. Caspen wrapped his hand around hers.

"My parents threatened to send me back to Navarin," Kayln claimed. "What we did was foolish. Fae have to be perfect all the time. We don't do such silly things."

Nalysse's eyes grew round as they spoke a million hate-filled, distasteful words at Kayln.

Meesha thwarted the fae/elf battle. "My parents aren't happy either. They said it was careless, especially as a lycan. At least I'd shifted back by the time Devan portalled me." Implying they'd be more angry had they known she shifted into a wolf as a distraction.

The conversation went into a self-pity spiral as they shared how much trouble they were in.

She didn't feel bad breaking up their mutual pity party. "I went back," Terra stated.

"You did what?" Caspen asked.

Terra guessed Hyacinth hadn't said anything. "I went back and brought the five with me. The adults were waiting when we returned and they're at a house in Provence."

"We have to go see them," Hyacinth stated.

On the way into town, Terra caught up to Hyacinth. Caspen walked ahead of her, talking with Kinzo. It was the only chance she might get. "How are the burns?"

"Better. Nearly gone. I didn't tell Caspen yet about what we figured out," she said it as if she felt guilty.

Terra didn't pry into that. He was protective of her, even though she was strong and independent. That was something they needed to figure out. There was something else Terra was curious about. "How did Devan find you last night?"

"It's a vampire ritual. Private, among families. When a new child is brought in, he or she drinks a drop of everyone in the family's blood and they drink a drop of the new child. It binds us together. We can always find each other and feel the other's emotions."

"So your parents also knew. That's why everyone's parents were waiting."

Hyacinth nodded.

The Land of Lost Souls

Terra took a deep breath for the next one. What she'd learned from the tribunal today would surely make Hyacinth feel worse, but she also felt she needed to know. "She's gone."

"Who?"

"The vampire. They sent a team back for her, but she was gone."

Hyacinth's eyes drained and her complexion grew lighter. "They moved her?"

"Maybe."

"It's all my fault." Guilt resounded in her words.

The evening sky in Provence was depressing as the fake sun lowered, colors like a painting spread across the sky, and the moon, real or fake she couldn't be sure, rose into the sky, stars twinkled, but every day looked exactly the same. "No. It's everyone's fault this is such a mess. They shouldn't have had you track her down, but you should have said something."

They reached the house. A two-story, dark green and camel-colored home. A troll answered the door. They agreed no guards, but insisted an adult be there with them. The troll, a female, opened the door and allowed them in, her orange tail plumage bright and cheerful as the smile on her face. Terra had brought some stuff from her kiosk. She figured Provence food wouldn't settle any better with them than it did her. She set her backpack on the table and was joined by Warlita.

"Food. The stuff they gave us for dinner was decent. It was different, but not bad," Warlita said as she pulled out a wooden chair and sat at the table.

Was it Terra? Everything she tried was horrible, except some of the fruit. "Really? I tried quite a few things before I gave up and they gave me my own kiosk at the school. If no one is hungry, I'll put the stuff in the freezer."

"Who said no one is hungry?" Alex said as he walked into the kitchen. She stuffed a tray of pizza bagels into the oven.

The group stayed for about an hour. They were being treated good.

On the way back, Terra waited for a chance to confront Nalysse but Kinzo was attached to her the entire time. It was hard to tell with them anymore if things were good or bad. Things looked good, but one never could tell with them. She didn't want to involve him, so returned to the dorm and waited before knocking on Nalysse's door.

In usual Terra-fashion, she didn't mince words. "You knew that formula wouldn't work."

Nalysse stepped into the hallway and closed the door behind her. "No, I didn't..." She shifted on her feet nervously.

"Yes, you did. There is no cure."

Her voice low, she nearly whispered, "I did know. The properties of the bungai leaf mixed with temani root salve take away the pain and symptoms for twenty-four hours before the vampire drops dead."

"Why would you do that?"

"I thought it would make Hyacinth feel as though we'd saved her and," she paused. "I can't figure out what went wrong. You should take your suspicions up with Kayln. She's the one that sprinkled stupid fairy dust into a delicate elfin recipe," Nalysse said with a bite to her words.

There was one more thing she had to get off her chest. She and Nalysse would never be best friends, but they were friends and she owed her the truth. "There's nothing between Kinzo and I. Never has been. He was my first friend in Provence and Clyde loves him."

Nalysse admitted, a sharp ring to her tone, "I've been a little jealous, but I know nothing is happening between the two of you."

The little talk they had didn't convince Terra that she didn't poison the vampire on purpose. Nalysse was too nervous. Either she was guilty, or she did something else. Fae always thought more of themselves, so Kayln adding fairy dust wasn't a shock. Maybe it was just the combination. She understood wanting to make Hyacinth happy but, no matter what the results, it wouldn't have had a good ending.

Clyde nudged his face against hers as she entered her dorm. The light was on and Halsey dropped a few dresses onto her bed, not even glancing at Terra.

Terra vaguely remembered going back to the dorm the previous day and Halsey being out. It was day 6, so no school. The past twenty-four hours had gone quickly, but she was sure Halsey hadn't been there. "You're back."

"You were worried?" Halsey asked.

"A little." Terra pinched her fingers together.

"Festival of dust. It's a celebration of the dead with the change of seasons. It's a requirement as Diama. The festival of colors celebrates new life."

The indifference in Halsey's tone alerted the hairs on Terra's arm to stand at attention. Something was different. As if she left Halsey as Halsey and came back to a different version. Halsey 2.0, and she wasn't sure if she liked her.

In Lols, Terina had a cracked veil in a closet inside a closet that led to a cave filled with fairy dust. She'd tucked the bottle away for safe keeping. "Does fairy dust come from caves?"

"No. It may gather in caves, but it's the gift of death. A fae turns into a pile of fairy dust; from there it blows into the air and is washed into the Lavender Seas."

Eww! Terra rubbed her hands against her pants, as she'd touched fairy dust without knowing it was the remains of a dead fae. "Does that still happen when a fae dies outside of Navarin?"

"No. The fae's spirit is trapped in their body and must be brought to Navarin immediately."

That rubbed Terra the wrong way. If it was so important for fae, why so many in Lols? "What about all the hybrid fae stuck in Lols?"

"I hadn't thought of that." The lack of empathy in her tone made Terra cringe.

Of course not. Why would she expect them to think about that, and what about other subspecies and their death rituals?

Her response was quick, but something in her tone was off as if she'd practiced it. "Tell me about it?" Terra scratched her arm. All day it had itched on and off, right at the bend of her left elbow. It was red from being scratched. In the middle was a tiny dot. Had she been bit by a bug? It had to have been in Lols, since Provence didn't have any biting bugs.

Halsey went on to describe a massive fae gathering that sounded like a PG Mardi Gras where fae wore fall's first leaf drops, flowers strung around their necks like beads.

Not once did Halsey look her in the eye which made Terra feel slighted. It wasn't Halsey alone but Nalysse too.

Classes seemed so boring after the past week. Her mind kept slipping back to seeing Noah. She'd hardly had any alone time with him. Mention of Serenity Tree brought her attention back to class.

"The Serenity Tree is life. It was the principal healing agent to all ailments in the early days. Jumaga created the first true elvin remedy, a serum made from mulp bulbs, teeple sprout, and water from Iridi river that directly feeds Serenity Tree," instructor Teantra explained.

A first-year elf, Adoren, raised her hand, "But some ailments still have no cure."

"Yes, science is working on those. It's a process."

Terra's mind drifted to Nalysse and her family's recipe for a lycan bite. Was there really no cure? Had her plan been to bring trouble upon her? Instead of asking in class, she waited for it to end and directly approached instructor Teantra.

With a smile, Teantra asked, "Did you have a question about the lesson?"

"Sort of. Are there elfin cures that are more secret?"

"It is possible. Each family throughout history has added recipes to the growing list. Some families may keep proprietary rights over theirs, such as fae do with spells. Is there a particular ailment?"

Terra shrugged. "Not really. I know something like a lycan bite is lethal to vampires. If a cure had ever been found, someone would know it right?" She didn't want to sound as if she was prying.

"A lycan bite is always lethal. There is no history of any known cure, but there are remedies that can make the death not as unpleasant."

The list of various ingredients they used came to mind and Terra asked about them. Maybe they were used to ease the symptoms, so the vampire's death was less unpleasant.

"Those are common for most ailments, except bungai leaf. It is only found in the forest of Maredam and was commonly used on the tip of an arrow against the enemy. It has no known healing properties, but causes paralysis, so is generally used as anesthesia."

Anesthesia would make sense. It would make the pain go away and supported Nalysse's story. Remembering how Kayln had sprinkled dust into the serum, she asked, "Does fairy dust have an effect on elfin remedies?"

"It can, but it depends on the intentions of the fairy and how strong they are with magic. They can accentuate a remedy or destroy it. In general, most fae spells on elfin remedies have little effect."

Terra thanked her instructor and let the information roll around in her head. She didn't think either Kayln or Nalysse had any ill intentions. She accepted Nalysse's story.

24

Bane couldn't believe his ears as M'ra asked him to give the young vampire in dire shape Terra's blood. In shock, he questioned her without thinking. As soon as the words left his lips he apologized.

"I chose you of all the vampires for this job because I trust you." M'ra's words reflected the hidden threat that, if you utter a word, you will die a horrible death. "Terra's blood is special. She contains life from every realm. If anything can save the girl, it is her blood."

Bane understood that meant Terra was… the one thing no one could speak of. Somehow, she escaped the cleansing and

M'ra's suspicions all these years were justified. Did it also mean that Cyrus was alive? Did he smuggle himself and her into Lols? Had he been hiding there, and were these creatures with lightning whips and blades some concoction of his power?

His brain stuck on that for several moments. She didn't go anywhere without the ferret. Cyrus was powerful; was he powerful enough to hide as a furry animal all these years?

He stuck a finger between the girl's blackening lips and drained the vial of blood, slowly as not to waste any, down the girl's throat. M'ra watched and together they waited.

He eased into the I-killed-someone-else in Lols conversation by giving M'ra the news on the blood sample he'd collected from the electric person. "The testers are done with the blood sample from Lols. They haven't identified what they are yet, but have narrowed down they're mortal with long life spans."

"Pureblood?"

"They believe so. I ran into more people with the electric ability. The woman who got away the first time, and a young man, no more than nineteen. I had to kill the woman, as she attacked me. He got away, but I got more blood, several samples from her.

They are testing them against those in the archive."

The veil over her face, he couldn't see her expression as she leaned back in her chair as if in thought. Was she thinking the same as him? That Cyrus was somehow behind them?

After class, Terra stopped by her dorm for the book. It was in her closet, in a box under her favorite boots, where she'd left it. It wasn't that she didn't trust Halsey, but she didn't trust Halsey. The other option she considered was visiting Rosette and leaving it there, but Halsey finding it was better than Rosette. She cringed at what Rosette would say if she knew she had an ancient fae book. It wasn't the Grimoire, but it was something.

Clyde clamored around her as she made her way to Gwond's. His class was out, as she'd expected. Without knocking on the door, he glanced up, his eyes large and bulgy under his glasses.

"Come in, Terra."

She dropped the backpack on one of the tables. "I went to Navarin."

His tail plumage rested on his shoulder. "And what did you find?"

She pulled the book out. "This. It's not the Grimoire. I'm not sure what it is."

He smiled. "There are many mysteries to the realms, as I'm sure your adventure taught you."

She wasn't sure which adventure he meant; Navarin or Lols. Surely, he'd heard or been told, since he was her instructor. "Yes…" It dawned on her in that moment that mysteries did abound. Her father had possession of a book that, according to Noah, contained information about the realms. "What do you know about a book titled 'The Origin'?"

His eyes grew wide under his glasses. "I've never heard of such a book." He studied her face. "It's not that one, but another?"

She nodded and leaned against the table. "I don't have it though."

"You know where it is?"

"Yeah. I do." But getting it would be more difficult now that she was on the tribunal's radar.

"Mysteries there are. How is your use of magic coming along?"

He was her magic instructor. She wasn't sure what to tell him. It seemed the longer she stayed in Provence the less she trusted others, or maybe it was that her use of magic was so strange and unlike anyone else's. She tried to believe it was because she was hybrid. Attempted to convince herself, but the more she did the less convinced she was. "Meesha's a good tutor."

"She is one of the best." He studied her face. "Is there something else?"

She wasn't sure how to say it, or if she should. What she and Kayln and Hyacinth figured out had stuck with her, but it seemed there was no one but them to talk to about it. "Is it possible for anyone to use magic to make sunlight?"

His plumage pulled the glasses off his eyes, and he rubbed them with his hand, then his plumage put them back on his face. "Not that's recorded in any book in Provence. A skill like that would be kept hidden."

Every discussion with Gwond left her curiouser. After leaving his office, Clyde was extra bouncy. He'd sat in class then she'd dragged him to Gwond's. It was time for him to run and be a ferret.

Clyde ran ahead of her, stretching his little legs as he always did as they walked into the woods behind the school. She sped her pace when he disappeared from her sight. "Clyde," she called. When he didn't bounce back to her immediately, she called again. That wasn't like him. Her heartbeat sped up and her throat became dry in worry. "Clyde!" She ran to where she'd seen him last.

A vampire stepped from the trees. She recognized him as the shady one who'd kidnapped Tania, in his designer suit and slicked short dark hair. The one who was kicked off the tribunal. In his arms was Clyde.

She proceeded with caution. "Thanks," she said as she approached.

His lips curled into a devious smile. "Don't thank me yet. I need you to come with me."

"I will not. Let him go!"

He chuckled. "He's my insurance policy."

Was that it? Kidnapping Tania didn't work out, so he was kidnapping her by taking Clyde hostage? What was it with him? "No. You'll give me back my ferret and go away."

Ignoring her, as she posed no threat to him, he turned on his heel. Clyde chittered angrily in his arms as he squirmed to get away.

Heat rose in Terra as anger bubbled to the surface. She rushed towards him. "He'll bite you!"

"I heal quickly."

His indignant voice prickled every one of her nerve endings. She had no choice but to follow him. Clyde was all the family she had.

"I'll be needing that," he said, pointing to her comicay.

25

The light sands, rocky low mountains, and crimson sky of Drakonia reminded her of the day she'd accidentally entered the realm. It was Clyde who went through the curtain first. At least from inside the tower she couldn't smell the metallic odor of the air from Blood River.

The door opened and Bane entered with a cage. Clyde peered at her through the slats.

Bane was a special sort of twisted vampire. Anger flushed her cheeks. "What are you doing? I'm here. This is what you asked. Give him back!" she demanded.

He ignored her and depressed his comicay. A hologram of someone with a dark veil over their head appeared. "Hello Terra," she said, in a sweet voice.

Terra wasn't feeling sweet, and their hospitality sucked rotten eggs. "What do you want?"

Bane chided, "No one speaks to the Minister that way."

No one speaks to the minister that way. She'd speak to her anyway she wanted. In forty-eight hours, she'd almost been eaten by vampires in Lols, found out her friend was held captive by ropes spelled with UV light, brought five hybrids from Lols, and now her ferret was kidnapped. "I'm not a vampire and you kidnapped Clyde. I'll talk any way I want."

The Minister chuckled, making Terra's blood boil. "You have that right, but you are of interest. By my count, you've entered seven of the eight realms. You must visit Thraves immediately."

By her count, what did that mean? Had she been tailing her? "Why?"

"Show her," she ordered Bane.

He slid a curtain back, revealing someone lying on a bed. Terra moved closer, noting her swollen face, glands, and black veins. "You..." The tribunal said she'd been taken, but Terra never thought the vampires did it. But why not? Why hadn't she naturally assumed that? Of course the girl was of interest to them. "Why?"

"You can save her."

"Me?" Terra snorted. "That's funny."

Terra couldn't see much under the veil, but she squared her shoulders which said she was serious. "You must go to Thraves and return, only then can you save her."

Her words made no sense. How did her going to Thraves help a vampire dying of a lycan bite? "I don't understand."

The burgundy back drop against the minister's dark veil and her grave words gave Terra the chills. "You will. Go to Thraves. Under Blood Falls is the curtain. Once you cross it, you must return immediately. The girl's time is limited."

Terra's mind spun. She barely knew what to do with her magic and now she was being asked to save someone's life by doing something that made zero sense. All she wanted was her ferret returned. "Alright, but only if Clyde can come with me."

Bane snorted. "He's our insurance. You'll get him when you return."

Terra crossed her arms in defiance. She had something they wanted, whether she understood why or not, and they had something she wanted. "Then I'm not going."

The minister replied in an annoyed tone: "Let her take the ferret. She will return."

Bane opened the door of the cage and let it drop. Clyde stared at him then Terra, as if unsure what to do. She opened her arms and he jumped towards her and into her arms. Maybe the minister wasn't as evil as she'd thought. Clyde nuzzled her neck as if they'd been apart for months.

In a teal flash, she was standing in front of the falls. Blood poured down the side of the mountain, falling into the river, and the metallic odor gave her a weird taste in her mouth.

"I'll be waiting," Bane said in an unpleasant, forceful voice.

Whatever. You can do this, Terra. "Ignore him," she whispered to Clyde. She held him close as she searched for a way to get under the falls without getting splashed with blood.

Finding a place where the blood was thinner on its descent and the river narrower, Terra decided it was the best place and they'd get the least blood-soaked. She cringed as she ducked under the falls in a place where she at least didn't have to step into the river. With a leap, she jumped across the falls to another rock.

Almost losing her balance, she put her arms out. Clyde crawled onto her shoulder and clung. After the quick falter, she regained her balance. Instead of turning around to go back immediately, she studied her surroundings.

The rock was much like Drakonia. In front of her was a cave. Had Tania come this way? She remembered the glowing stalactites

Tania found and wondered how far into the caves she had to go to find one of her own. Her curiosity taking the front seat, she walked into the cave, allowing her 3D map mind to chart a path.

The cave wound downhill. At the end was a stream of fresh water. She followed it. Clyde scurried down her and scooted ahead, poking his nose into a hole in the rock. "What are you doing? Who knows what lives in this cave?" She suddenly got a chill thinking about it.

She leaned down to collect Clyde and saw what he was after. Something shiny inside the hole glowed. She glanced around for something to pull it out. In the stream was a branch. She grabbed it and poked it inside the hole. She moved it to the side of the object and pushed. It budged. She continued until the glowing, violet-white ball was radiating in front of her. Not sure what it was, or if she should touch it, she dropped her backpack and pushed it inside. Clyde chittered loudly as she did.

"It's not a toy, but we'll take it back with us and find out what it is." Surely someone would know. There weren't many harvesters in Provence but there were a couple she'd seen around Provence Academy.

He chattered more in protest. Collecting him in her arms, she said, "We have to go back." Not that she wanted to, but had to. If she didn't, there was no doubt in her mind the vampires would make sure to take care of her in a unpleasant way.

Bane didn't looked like he'd moved in the short time she was gone, except for the grumpier expression on his face.

"That took long enough," he mumbled under his breath. Without another word, he opened a portal. The teal light swirled, warm and inviting.

The light dropped her off in the same tower, noted by the view from the window. Two soft velvet chairs and a dark wooden table between them. A wall in this room had a picture of somewhere in Drakonia, noted by the light sand and winding, red river.

A vampire entered the room, a female with scrubs. That was a first. Her long hair tied up in a hairnet. A vampire phlebotomist; she chuckled subconsciously at her own joke.

"Follow me," the vampire said in a perky voice as she opened the door to another room.

She followed her into the room with the sick vampire. The girl looked worse up close. Dark lines webbing her swollen face. A second, identical bed was parallel to it, a couple feet between them. The night the vampire in her cat form stalked them in Canida, Terra had been terrified, and now the poor girl was a shadow of that magnificent creature.

The Land of Lost Souls

The phlebotomist slid the curtain back on a window between the rooms.

"Lay down and hold your arm out."

Her body tensed as she sat on the bed and lowered her arm. She hated needles and never looked when given vaccines.

The vampire pulled a chair between the beds then tapped her vein and delicately put the syringe into her arm.

Terra cringed. She hated giving blood and getting shots. From the corner of her eye, she watched a flow of blood snake through the tube connecting her to the other vampire. Pulling her eyes away, she searched for Clyde but didn't need to search far as his paws and face were against the glass between the rooms.

After what felt like several minutes, Terra got a bit nervous. She only had so much blood in her body and preferred to keep as much as possible. "Are you leaving me any?"

The vampire didn't respond, and Terra suddenly grew nervous. Did they have to drain her to save the vampire? "I think you've taken enough," Terra said forcefully.

The phlebotomist smiled. "Not yet."

She wanted to wipe the smile off her face. Her eyes drifted to her scrubs. A tag read 'June'. That fit her perky, smiley-faced personality that was grating on Terra's nerves. "I'd like to keep enough blood to continue my first life," Terra snarked.

June responded, "You will."

Terra woke up, discombobulated, as she hadn't remembered going to sleep. She was still on the bed, but in another room. Its walls dark green. She rolled her head to the right, noting the vampire, Bane, in a chair a few feet away. He had one leg crossed over another.

Panic struck her when she didn't see Clyde. She lifted up on her elbows to get a better look. "Where is he?"

Bane asked in a nonchalant tone, "Who?"

Panicked, she yelled, "Clyde! What did you do with him?"

Bane finally glanced her way. "He's with Minister M'ra."

That didn't make her feel any better. She wasn't at all sure about her. She pulled her legs over the bed. "I'm done. I want him here, and I want to leave."

"You need to eat."

She'd lost so much blood she'd passed out, the minister had her ferret and was going to do who knows what. Desperately, she wanted out of the nightmare but, judging by Bane's expression, she wasn't going anywhere soon. "Fine. I'll take a cheeseburger with loaded cheese fries, and Clyde eats with me. He needs ferret food."

Bane didn't acknowledge her words as he left the room. A few minutes later, the door opened and Clyde ran in. He stood on his hind legs and sniffed then, finding her, bounded to her and climbed all over her.

"I missed you too."

After they'd reunited, a vampire in a black suit brought a tray in. He moved his hands and legs dropped from the bottom. He placed it in front of her and lifted the lid on a large plate then the lid on another containing a small bowl filled with ferret pellets and water. "Orange or cranberry juice?" he asked.

Neither went with the meal in front of her. It was exactly what she'd asked for and it smelled delicious. Cheese melted over the fries, hunks of bacon and scallions drizzled over the sides. "Cranberry and can I get water?"

Within minutes, he returned with a glass of red liquid and another with ice and water. "Why juice?" she asked.

"The Minister's orders." He left her there, alone with Clyde and the amazing meal in front of her. It was loaded with carbs. She hadn't any idea what time it was. The room didn't have a window or a clock. She took the bowl and placed it beside her. Clyde clamored up the bed and ate.

Tania's experience here hadn't been so great from what she said. Why was she being treated like royalty? While she ate, Clyde munched on his dinner then, as if the food was loaded with batteries, he jumped off the bed and ran circles around the room.

She was full and ready to go home and lie in her bed at the dorms.

A teal light flashed at the edge of her bed and the woman in the veil, Minister M'ra, appeared when the light dissipated. Not hiding behind a holocall; she was there in person. She remembered at the tribunal meeting when she challenged them that Minister M'ra hadn't shown up at all, she sent Devan and spoke through him. Why was Terra important enough for her to show herself? Was it because Terra posed no threat?

M'ra lifted the veil over her face, her hair still covered. She reminded Terra of someone, as she studied her face and features. It wasn't like she was exceptionally beautiful, but was attractive in her own right. Terra couldn't quite make out her eye color, but her face was oval. She wasn't any taller than Terra, with a medium build.

Terra pushed the tray aside and swung her legs over the bed.

"She's going to make it."

That was great, especially since she'd given up so much blood. "How is my blood a cure?"

M'ra traced the bed frame with a manicured finger. "How do you feel?" she asked, ignoring Terra's question.

"I'm full. How am I a cure for a lycan bite? How did you know?"

"I have lived a very long life." She paused for a minute. "A couple different lives before this one. I know many things. It is best you don't tell anyone about this."

Only an idiot would tell people they were the cure for a lycan bite. "I'm sure someone is wondering where I am."

M'ra smiled. "We've taken care of that. You are unique. Once the passport embeds, you will see more than you've ever seen. You will feel the movement around you. You will be able to mold it."

Mold it. The words bounced in her head. She already felt she could, but couldn't figure out how. "What are you talking about?"

A teal light enveloped M'ra and she vanished without giving her an answer.

Bane returned; his face solemn. The only time she'd seen him smile was when he was doing something rotten like kidnapping Clyde. "Are you ready?"

"To go home? More than ready."

His lips curled. *Uh oh, what evil was hatching in his brain?* "You are the only one in all the realms that can enter all eight."

She swallowed.

26

Concentration was difficult, as Terra's mind wandered and replayed M'ra's words. It made her head hurt. After class, she took Clyde for a walk. She was sure to put him on his harness. Then she sat beneath a tree and caught up on her homework. She didn't have to complete the work when she was absent on tribunal business, but chose to or she'd be more lost than she already was.

At dinner, she noted tension between Kinzo and Nalysse. They didn't stroll in together and barely looked the other's way. She wanted to tell them about her experience but considered M'ra's warning. For the time being, she decided to keep it secret. In fact, she wanted to push all the craziness from the past several weeks aside and be a teen, a senior enjoying her last year of high school. She thought of Noah. All she had to do to talk to him was enter the fourth floor of Provence Academy. That's how close Lols was to her.

The passport hadn't inked yet. Usually, it happened within a day. She expected it anytime and decided her dorm was the best place. She'd chill in her PJs and wait.

She dropped her heavy backpack onto her bed. It was gaining weight each day. She unzipped it and noted the glowing sphere and the old book. She placed the book back in the box in her closet and rolled the sphere into the box. It settled beside the book. She closed the lid and set her boots back on top.

It was only moments after dropping an oversized T-shirt over her shoulders, the door opened and Halsey walked in.

Without making eye contact she strolled to her closet. "How was Lols?" she asked.

"Home. I miss it."

Halsey slid clothes and pushed them in various directions as she studied the department store of clothing in her closet. "Oh."

"What is it?" Terra asked. Halsey was odd and fae, but this was even more odd than usual and not exactly entitled Diama fae. *I'm better than everyone.*

Halsey spun around, shoving something behind her back. Her lips teased a smile.

"What?" Terra said, sharper than she expected.

Halsey brought her hands forward. "I got it!" she said, a rolled parchment-type paper with a string around the middle in her hands.

The spell book. She got Merla's Realm Grimoire book. "How did you?"

"The other book was a map. I know I shouldn't have, but don't be mad. I found it in your closet and returned it once I translated it then went to Navarin and followed the map."

Halsey wasn't that adventurous alone. She remembered how she didn't want to enter the sea cave and how she made a big deal about getting the key to the fourth floor of the school and how she insisted on not leaving the Lols side Provence Academy and Meesha stayed with her. "Who helped you?"

"Bjorn."

Of all people. How did they manage to work together and follow the map without killing each other?

As if Halsey read her expression of shock she said, "He's not that bad."

The smile on her face and dreamy far off look in her eye, not to mention how oddly

not-Halsey she was acting, she was sure
something had happened between them.
Sparks of romance. "Ohh, you and Bjorn."

She clasped her manicured hands in
front of her. "It's nothing. I'm the Diama. We
had fun."

Terra was more interested in their
adventure than the spell scroll at the moment.
Halsey brought the scroll to Terra and
dropped it on her lap.

She picked it up. Holding it gave her
the chills. The scroll with the level four magic
spell that created the veils between the realms.
It was possibly the most dangerous written
word in any of the realms. The gravity of what
she had finally hit her.

27

Hank consciously attempted to keep his nervous foot from tapping as he waited for the regional Wizard, the head of the Northeast Regional Warlocks. He'd run to escape the vampire, fearing for his own life. Guilt ate him up that he couldn't do anything to stop him. At the same time, Juwel ran after her other partner died, so he dreaded punishment.

He'd gone back to the house the next day. The girl with the energy trails, the one they were searching for, went into the large house. Outside was overgrown with weeds and heavy, unruly vines climbed the house. Inside it was dusty and musky. All the curtains closed downstairs, there was no light or power. As a warlock, that wasn't a problem.

He infused the house with enough electricity to snoop around.

At eighteen, almost nineteen, he'd been out of warlock school for a few months. His powers were still emerging and would continue with each passing assignment. At this point, he wasn't powerful enough to handle it alone. Going alone was commonplace anyways. He traced the plasma rune on his arm. His first one he'd received. Since then, he'd gained a few more. They always burned like a brand with a hot poker.

What he found inside the house was nothing until he got to the fourth floor. The door leading up was the only locked door inside the house. All he saw was a vacant, unpainted, boring room until he glanced outside the windows. Flabbergasted, he stepped backwards in shock, unable to comprehend what he was seeing. Silver, lavender, blue, and green leafed trees and colorful, well-manicured flora.

Teenagers everywhere, in a courtyard that looked like something from a fairytale, and holding hands as they walked through the wooded area. He ran to a window across the giant room. More colorful flora and a water fountain. A statue of a dragon in the center. He'd gulped, unsure what to make of any of it. Had he stumbled on the land stolen from the warlocks all those years ago?

Realm Walker

More mysterious than viewing was when he opened the door that brought him to the room to go downstairs and visit this new land it brought him back to where he started. Eventually, he found a back door but, even with his magic, was unable to unlock it. That set him on his next journey of tracing the girl's steps. It seemed he was the only warlock that could see the energy surrounding her. It followed her like a comet's tail.

There was enough left he was able to retrace some of her steps, finding something more mysterious than the hidden land. She'd found other realms; one with beautiful green trees and plants, and huge, colorful gems jutting from the earth. Large, colorful birds buried their heads in his presence as if to hide, their tails covered in bright plumage.

Another took him to a snow-covered, mountainous land. He'd have stayed longer, except a white dragon with a wingspan larger than its body soared over him. Not wanting to get eaten or discovered, he returned.

What he didn't find was the artifact that triggered the search for the girl. At first, they hadn't known which of the group of teens triggered it. Not until she returned. The artifact was one of two the warlocks had spent centuries searching for. Her touch awakened the magic. By the time the warlocks got there, the artifact was gone, and its signature hidden again. She didn't have it. He was sure of that, and was reluctant to say anything about the house and the hidden world.

A door slid open, and a woman dressed in a silver gown, her head covered with a silver hat that looked something like a papal tiara, entered. He knelt, as she was the regional warlock.

She took a seat in the large, throned chair made from a gold alloy. "You may stand."

Her features noted her age. Small lines webbed from her brown eyes and over her cheeks. A flab of loose skin made for a second chin.

As commanded, he stood.

"I hear you found another world?"

He nodded nervously. "Yes. It is beautiful and diverse with life entirely different than Lols. I feel it may be the lost realm stolen from us."

She folded her hands in her lap. The floppy sleeves on her arms spreading against the arms of the throne. "Hmm… How did you find this hidden realm?'

He swallowed, careful what slipped off his tongue. "In the search for the artifact, which I didn't find. It had been moved already. Its energy masked, I found a portal. When I walked through it, it took me to a beautiful land covered in huge gemstones. The artifact had definitely been there, and an energy signature was left which I followed until it vanished to other lands. I think they may all be one and the same."

"What you've told me is useful. You have a special knack. Have you another rune?"

"No."

"Interesting. The guard will be getting in touch with you. I have a special mission that it seems only you can do as no one else lives or sees the same energy signatures. Tell me what, exactly, do you see?"

He responded, choosing his words carefully and not involving the girl. "Shifting energy and colorful trails in the air."

"Very well. Juwel was unfortunate, but you will serve no punishment. I want to know more about this vampire. Have they broken our centuries long pact," she lifted her neatly trimmed triangle brows, "or are they from this other world you found?"

"He's very strong. I only saw his face for a moment. His features were fine and pretty, medium build, medium height. His clothes were expensive. Ruthless, he was ruthless, lacked fear of the UV in our beams, even though they burned him. They had little impact but to upset him more. He wanted to know what we were doing. We didn't tell him anything and the girl doesn't seem of much interest." He swallowed hard as he'd just lied to the regional wizard. He hoped she didn't notice how nervous he was, as he'd been nervous and had a hard time stopping his foot from tapping. Without Juwel alive there was no one to say otherwise.

"You may go."

He stepped back and bowed before exiting through the guarded door.

28

Warlock Council Chamber

The Regional Wizard, Latisha, stood as the Northeastern Werewolf pack leader and Northeastern Vampire Clan leader took their seats at the long table. Each brought their warriors. She also had hers. It wasn't often they met, other than their yearly council meeting.

Hank was a superior warlock and didn't seem to have that understanding. She placed him with one of the most skilled warlocks, who was to keep a close eye on him, as she felt he was developing the source rune. A much-coveted rune that hadn't appeared for centuries.

She turned her attention to the curious crowd of vampires and werewolves.

They hated one another, more so since the werewolf-bit vampire was discovered, yet all of them had something in common. "Thank you for meeting with me. I understand there is much tension but, once you hear what I have to say, you may find we all have a common enemy."

The pack leader scoffed as he rubbed a thick thumb beneath his chin. Testosterone. Why were wolves so misogynistic? The vampires were so much more refined and easier to work with. Ignoring his jeer, she continued, turning her attention to the vampires, "The wolf that bit one of your youths may not have been of this realm."

From the corner of her eye, she watched the wolf's attention perk at her comment. "A young warlock discovered portals into another realm and had a run in with a powerful vampire unabated by our UV."

Now she had both their attention. "Where are these portals?" asked the vampire clan leader, Hiram. His vibrant blue eyes met her gaze.

"We have designed a map with the young warlock's help. They are everywhere. We've sent teams on exploratory missions. What we've found is this not a single realm but many."

The pack leader, Winston, always alpha and always skeptical, folded his arms over his chest as he flashed a hateful glance at Hiram. "You're saying the vampire isn't of this realm, nor the wolf that attacked the young vampire?"

She ignored his sneer. Her revelation meant it wasn't one of his, as previously suspected. She responded, "Exactly."

"When do we visit these *realms?*" Winston asked.

With the need to put him in his place, she responded, "Don't get ahead of yourself. First, we need a truce. Once that is established, we can move forward with a plan."

To be continued…

Hidden Passages
REALM WALKER VOL. 2

1

Northeastern Regional Wizard

Latisha shuddered with a pinched face as she closed the periwinkle blue curtains. The dark nymphs, with their razor-sharp teeth, springs of unkempt hair that stood out at all angles, were the most disgusting creatures she'd ever seen. She understood why they stayed hidden and were the creatures of most human childhood nightmares.

They weren't more than two inches in height, but carried the stench of rotting flesh. Stuffing a rag to her nose, she reached under the sink and sprayed her quarters with air freshener.

Dropping the rag from her nose, she stuffed it into the laundry chute by the long, silver dresser. Latisha couldn't sit still as she paced from one end of her private quarters to the other. A velvet chaise, the color of periwinkle, sat beneath a large window below the curtains she'd pulled shut. The recessed lights decreased in brightness as she turned the knob to help her focus by limiting distractions.

All shades of blue pillows were laid against the headboard of the silver bed frame. The bed made to perfection, with zero wrinkles. The other end of the room housed her massive closet. Through the closet, a door was built into a fake wall that led to her office and their formal meeting room.

She clenched her fists then released as she let out a deep breath. She could almost smell Marsidia. The Stones of Hovrath were last in the fae lands, and they were finally taking them back. Warlocks had waited so long and now she could taste it. The light at the end of the tunnel within reach, but a lot could go wrong and she didn't completely trust her sources.

Dark nymphs weren't reliable, but they were tiny enough to slip through the veil, undetected and undeterred. There were small gaps and cracks. The map they drew, and their intel, matched the stories of her ancestors. Their intel filled with the secrets of the other species. It was their weaknesses Latisha found most helpful, especially the larger and more vicious species.

The Land of Lost Souls

She had warlocks with the sun rune waiting for her command if there was any vampire trouble. They wouldn't create enough to fry every vampire, but would be able to send a powerful message and, if the warlocks banded together, they could shine as bright as the sun for a limited amount of time.

She didn't fool herself; the large and vicious species were a threat, but so were the others. All her forces carried silver swords should wolves become a problem and, according to the nymphs, vampire blood killed dragons.

Even the lesser species she took care of. Iron bullets would take out a fae and dreadwood grenades would subdue the elves. Dreadwood didn't grow on Earth, but the nymphs were helpful enough to bring some back, concentrated; and could do some damage.

The weapon that made her laugh was the water machine guns and rounds made of concentrated seawater to melt the trolls' skin off their short, squat little bodies. It wasn't her plan to use any weapons, but she never went in unprepared.

The nymphs asked only for passage to Marsidia. It was a small gift for all their intel. She hoped she didn't regret the decision later, as dark nymphs were known to stir trouble.

The wild card, she figured, were the wolves. They were a hotheaded group, making them untrustworthy and likely not to follow orders. To get them onboard, she had to give them something. Winston wanted land and a pact that neither warlocks nor vampires could cross onto their lands. There'd be consequences if they did. That demand didn't make her skin crawl, it was the other demand – give them the ability to shift at will without pain.

Only the eldest werewolves had the ability to shift on command without excruciating pain. Younger werewolves lacked that control; the phases of the moon controlling their shift. Under full and new moons, they shifted completely, and at other times of the month, a partial shift. All shifts caused discomfort at the least, and pain at the worst.

Hiram readily agreed, for if it wasn't for the warlocks the vampires would still be in the dark ages, only able to come out at night. The agreement the warlocks made with the vampires had proved fruitful over the years and their relationship grew, but she wasn't naïve enough to believe Hiram wouldn't go behind her back for the health of the vampire clans.

A team of adult warlocks with the invisibility rune waited on her command. Latisha's dark eyes glanced to the clock, and she let out a deep, sluggish breath. Her double chin bounced like jelly with the movement.

The Land of Lost Souls

Why did the clock move so slowly when waiting? The plan was to surround the fae on each side and take back what was stolen from the warlocks centuries ago. She wanted them to pay.

The approach was three-pronged, and all teams would enter at the same moment. Warlocks with the invisibility rune would enter the land of the elves, vampires the land of the fae, and wolves the land of trolls. In her long life, she'd only dreamt of this moment.

It was that blood boiling vengeance that led her to trust Hiram to extract information from the fae. The vampires' ability to manipulate the mind was superior to the warlocks'. It was as if it was part of the vampire by design.

The vampires weren't clouded by vengeance or anger. If she'd have sent in warlocks with the telepath rune, their judgements may have been blinded with anger, making them less effective in prying information and more likely to kill. She didn't necessarily want all the fae dead, at least not until they suffered. It was the Stones of Hovrath and safe passage to Marsidia for all warlocks who chose to return to their ancestral home that she yearned for so much she could taste the sweetness in the back of her throat.

Realm Walker

She had no ill will toward the elves or trolls. The warlocks and wolves were sent merely to secure the border, so none escaped.

With a circular wave of her hand, she watched as her warlocks struck the weak veil of the realm with lightning. She doubted a single elf would notice, as the lightning was concentrated to one area, then spread high above their clouds.

Northeastern Pack Leader

Winston wasn't sold on the plan or the pact between the wolves, warlocks, and vampires. He'd take the land if Latisha came through, but didn't trust her. Control over shifting he'd thrown in for good measure, and she'd agreed. He laughed inwardly, as she understood so little about his kind. Wolves weren't weak; it was the pain every change of the moon's cycle that gave them strength, honor, and courage.

His true solace was the confirmation that one of his wolves hadn't bitten the young vampire, as he'd insisted from the beginning. Rage burned inside him, his wolf begging to come out. Whoever these other creatures were, they had no business in his territory and causing his pack strife. How dare a wolf in another realm bite a vampire?! He tempered his rage. It would do him no good, not yet, and when all was done his wolves would be released from the curse of the moon. They'd have the freedom and land to shift and hunt at will.

As the alpha, he couldn't deny the existence of the other realms and the threat they posed. How dare they travel to and from his realm? It was high time these other realms understood exactly who they were dealing with. He wanted a piece of them, especially the vampires. To sink his own teeth into one and watch as the poison from his bite blackened their veins and swelled their face and extremities.

His wolves, men and women, heads held high, shoulders squared, looked upon him. Tonight, the other realms would know his kind – Earth kind – existed. Light energy hissed and cracked from the palms of warlocks, creating a portal. A warlock stretched the portal so it was large enough an army of wolves could slip in under the cover of night and position themselves to secure the border.

With pride, he watched as his wolves filed into the other realm.

The fae weren't his concern. The vampires were and, now that they were inside these mystery realms, he'd find a way to get to the vampires. The map, although incomplete, of these realms showed the vampire realm was close. He sent a small team of his best soldiers to find it.

He flashed his emerald eyes at Ryoni and slicked a hand through his dirty blonde hair. Ryoni gave a short nod as she and four others hung back. The warlock stayed by Winston's side. He was needed to open a portal back to Earth, but Winston knew he was also a spy for Latisha, the warlocks' regional wizard.

Each member of the pack had a job, and all were loyal to Winston. If the warlock became a problem, they'd take care of it.

Northeastern Clan Leader

The allegiance between the warlocks and vampires was fruitful. It was warlock spells that allowed vampires to walk in the daylight and live freely among the humans. The vampires in the other realm were weak to sunlight, according to the young warlock. It was also reported the land was flowing in blood – human blood.

Hiram swept a chunk of dark hair from his forehead as he leaned over the partial map of the fae realm. His vampires could walk in the sun, allowing them an advantage over other vampires. They would overtake a land of islands and lavender oceans. It was imperative to stay in line with the warlocks, as he wanted a truce with the vampire realm.

It was give and take. He gave Latisha what she wanted with the fae, and he could work a deal with the other vampire leader. He'd promise that leader the ability to walk in the sun, and his vampires would be able to come and go freely.

"We should portal directly to the palace, to the dungeon," Freya said as she studied the same incomplete map of the fae realm. She smoothed her hands over the body-hugging jogging pants covering her legs.

The map of the realm incomplete, they had a solid map of the palace, including how the beings in that realm were working on a potion to seal the veils between Lols and the other realms. Lols – an odd name for Earth.

It was that information bringing them to where they were now. The veils were the invisible barriers between the realms. The plan was to study the realms long enough to learn about the creatures, magic, customs, and build complete maps, but they no longer had that luxury. This had to be done before they were shut out forever.

Hiram lifted his eyes from the map. "Make sure you cover all the exits." He met Freya's eyes. She was a warrior, one of the best. He shifted his gaze to Grayson. His salt and pepper hair tied back neatly, his long ponytail falling over his shoulder. "When you get the all clear from Freya's team, you will portal into the King and Queen's chamber and secure them."

Grayson nodded. He had the uncanny ability to interrogate with his mind. The plan wasn't to harm the King and Queen, at least not yet. It was to pry information from them. Grayson wouldn't be alone; as he hijacked their minds, cat shifters would infiltrate the rest of the palace, meeting Freya's team halfway until it was secure.

2

Clyde scampered up the tree and flew off, tackling the chimu. They rolled to a stop at the porch steps, where Terra sat on a porch swing. Chimu were nearly the same size as a ferret, but had a face more like a house cat.

Terra glanced away from Clyde for a second to take the hot chocolate Rosette handed her. Rosette made good on her promise to bring Terra to Meradin Woods in Aradia. It had real seasons and, in the middle of fall, the breeze was chilly and felt good against Terra's skin. The air mingled with the scents from many different plants. It was sweet and fresh.

Rosette even made sure to bring commoner food for Terra to eat, instead of forcing vegetarian elf delicacies on her. Tiny white marshmallows floated on the top of the hot chocolate, surrounded by a frothy cream. She lifted the mug to her lips. Steam rose into her nostrils, causing her to glance again at the drink. It bubbled wildly, as if boiling on a stove.

Weird. A minute ago, it hadn't been boiling. Studying the drink, she couldn't figure it out. Rosette was drinking tea; not boiling tea, but hot tea. She set the cup on the table between her and Rosette to give it time to cool as she focused again on Clyde.

"He's made a friend," Rosette noted out loud.

"He's made a family of friends," Terra corrected, as the ferret and three chimu rolled together on the bluish-colored grass. Some trees in Aradia dropped their leaves, while others were evergreen, but not like the spiky evergreens in Lols. These had soft leaves, actual leaves. The leaves changing color were brilliant in crimson red, royal blue, and deep purple. Mixed with the leaves that didn't change, the woods were filled with color.

Bushes bloomed around the trees in similar colors and, at night, the sarcantha flowers made a showy, glowing display of blue. She remembered them from the elf party she crashed a few weeks ago. In Provence, everything would look as it did when they left yesterday. By Monday, when they returned, there'd be no change. No colorful leaves, glowing flowers, fresh air. She sighed.

It was still early as the sun dropped behind the trees. "Is this where you and my mom played?" Terra asked, remembering the memories Rosette shared from her comicay — a gel-like communication device they wore above their wrist.

"It is. Those trees went on endlessly. We'd run through them." Her face suddenly lit up like a little girl. "If we go now, I can show you something more beautiful." Rosette stood, excitement in her voice.

Terra glanced at her hot chocolate that was no longer boiling. She'd drink it cold when they returned. Rosette took her through the woods. Under the trees, green and yellow mushrooms gave off light similar to the sarcantha, but not as bright.

The trail through the woods went up a small rolling hill overlooking a brook. The sky colors matched the leaves and blended over the water in a breathtaking display. Various colors of leaves and flower petals floated on the surface of the water, moving with the current. Beyond the beauty in front of her, something else caught her eye. A stretch of thick trees, their leaves green and flopping over one another. "What's over there?" she asked, pointing.

"You can see that?" Rosette asked, raising a brow.

Sometimes she forgot, as a hybrid elf that was also dragon and some other things, she had acute vision. "Predator genes." The predator subspecies were the dragons, vampires, and lycans.

Rosette's face pinched. "It's the darklands. No one has gone there for centuries, but it's said the first elves to settle in Aradia lived there." There was something in her voice that said she was holding back.

What was she holding back? A high school rendezvous with a bad boy elf? Rosette was so uptight, Terra had a difficult time seeing her as a teen even though she'd seen pictures from her comicay. "Were you ever tempted?"

"Not me," Rosette spat out as if guilty.

Terra didn't linger. If it was a place no one went to, it was the kind of place she wanted to visit. It also gave her other ideas. According to Rosette, her family found her mom in Meradin Woods as a baby. She was a hybrid, part elf and part… Terra wasn't sure. The residents of the realms didn't, and don't, like hybrids. Rosette's family took in Terra's mom, raised her as their own. "Could my mom have been from there?"

Rosette thought for a moment, as if figuring out how to respond. "I don't think so." She patted the bottom of her large, bat-wing hair. It cast a shadow on the grass behind her.

Terra focused her vision on the darklands. Not her normal vision, but the one that allowed her to see things others couldn't. The maps she saw were becoming more detailed and dimensional. In the beginning, she saw gridded maps. Today she saw massive tree trunks, thick as a sequoia. Huge thorns and sticky brambles surrounded the woods as if to keep elves out.

The Land of Lost Souls

No matter how much effort she put in, she wasn't able to see inside the forest. Beyond the forest was Navarin – realm of the fae. The golden sky over the sea was barely visible. Terra wasn't too anxious to ever return. The lavender-colored seas and seafoam green sand were pretty at first, but after several minutes they were nauseating and the yippy doglike energy from the realm, coupled with the colors, was enough to turn her stomach. Aradia had soft energy, like a cat's purr.

Clyde had ridden her shoulder there, worn out from playing with the chimu. He rested his head beneath her chin as the last of the sun lowered beneath the horizon. Solaflies sparkled from the trees, but stayed hidden in the brush. A few weeks ago, they were everywhere. Maybe they didn't like the cold. Terra wrapped her arms around her chest.

Spending the weekend with Rosette hadn't been so bad. In Provence, the tribunal decided to allow the commoners, or humans, Terra brought from the Land of Lost Souls, or Lols for short, to stay and attend Provence Academy so they could learn about the realms and how to be tribunal diplomats. Lols was the only realm not represented and Terra thought to change that.

Terra herself was from Lols. She hadn't learned of the realms, or any of the subspecies, until her father passed. Not a day went by she didn't think of him. He was a fire dragon and her mom a hybrid who passed as an elf. According to Rosette, they escaped to Lols when Terra's mom got pregnant with her.

Every time thoughts of her mom entered her head, she thought of the pink carnation tattoo on her ankle and faux pains stabbed at her. It was there to represent the love from the mom she never knew. Nostalgic thoughts were interrupted when she suddenly felt dizzy and stumbled as if drunk, followed by a pain that shot over her torso.

The sky suddenly turned dark, and steaks of blue and violet lightning spread over it, crackling from one end to the next. Instinctively, she opened her predator vision and watched in horror and agony as the veils in the lower realms of Aradia, Verboten, and Navarin appeared to split wide open.

She dropped in pain. Clyde ran up to her knees and lifted his front paws as he sniffed at her face.

"Terra," Rosette's voice broke through the fog in her brain. "What's happening? Are you OK?" Honest concern flowing in her words.

"I'm…" No, she wasn't OK, and didn't understand what was happening. Is this what M'ra warned her of when she said she'd gain powers after collecting the last passport? She bore a passport to each realm on her chest. As bad as they hurt when they inked, the pain she felt with them was minute in comparison to the crippling weight on her now. "Do you see it?"

"See what?" Rosette asked, her voice shaking.

A muffle of voices Terra couldn't decipher flowed into her ears and two arms collected her and held her like a baby. She opened her eyes, not realizing she'd closed them, and stared into a pair of familiar, yet unfamiliar, eyes.

She woke on the couch in the trella, which was the elfin word for a log cabin as far as Terra could tell. The soft fabric beneath her, she rolled into the pillow behind her head, unsure what happened.

"Are you feeling better?" asked a male voice that sounded as if it was hovering above her.

She turned toward it and blinked. A thick dark-bearded man stared down at her. She sat up, suddenly alarmed, and stared wide-eyed at the elf. His pointed ear tips visible through the long, dark hair on his head woven into a braid. He wore the longest beard she'd ever seen. It hung from his face and stretched to his knees.

She swallowed. "Where's Rosette?" Every bone and nerve in her body suddenly tense.

"Calm down," he reassured her in a sincere voice, meant to soothe her nerves.

Something about him made every hair on her body hackle like a cat. "Where's Clyde?"

Upon hearing his name, Clyde's masked face peered at her over the top of the couch cushions. Terra let out a breath she didn't know she was holding, and opened her arms to the ferret, who crawled into her lap and sat. He wasn't a lap ferret. She didn't think there was such a thing. His little head moved in the direction of the man and his little body tensed. It was as if he was protecting her.

"I'm Kelon. You fainted. I carried you home." His voice soft and reassuring, but there was something odd about him. On the other hand, it seemed she'd met him before.

She studied him for a moment, attempting to figure out what was so off about him. He clearly looked like any elf. No. No, he didn't. It hadn't hit her until that moment. She studied his eyes. They went from jade to shades of blue and back to jade. She'd never seen an elf with hazel eyes; shades of blue and occasionally green like her friend, Nalysse, but never hazel, unless he was a hybrid. "I'm fine. You can go now."

His brows lowered in confusion at her hostile words. "Your reputation precedes you."

What was that supposed to mean? She rolled her eyes and pulled Clyde to her chest. "Seriously, you can go. The door is over there." She pointed.

He raked a hand from mouth to chest through his massive beard and pinched his face. "I should wait for your aunt."

"Suit yourself," Terra snapped, keeping an eye on him. Her mind rolling over what was off until she figured it out. His energy wasn't smooth like the cat's purr of Aradia, but more tense, like a rubber band being stretched. Elves generally radiated a similar energy to their realm. His energy was in conflict with the realm.

His mannerisms ate at her brain. They were familiar; how he raked his hand through his beard and peered at her from under the lose strands of hair on his face, yet she couldn't place him and was positive she didn't remember meeting him.

"We have to go," Rosette's firm voice interrupted the friction in the room. As if she felt it too, she halted in the entry way from the hall to the family room. Her eyes shifting from Terra to Kelon. "The realms have been breached."

Her words took a moment to sink in as Terra's mind connected the dots. That's what she felt! Terra glanced at Kelon for his reaction. It didn't convince her, as he cupped his hands over his mouth in mock surprise and, for a brief moment, his form appeared to shift like static. Terra blinked her eyes, then continued her visual exam of Kelon, noting he now looked quite normal.